Photo: John Borthwick

Merlinda Bobis is a Filipino bilingual writer now living in Australia. She has published three books of poetry, the third of which she has performed as theatre, with dance and chanting, on some twenty-five occasions in the Philippines, Australia, France and China. Her poems and short stories have appeared in Australian and Philippine journals and magazines. She is the author of a set of plays, *War Trilogy:* the first play, *Ms. Serena Serenata*, was performed at Sydney's Belvoir Street Theatre in 1997; the second, *Rita's Lullaby*, won the Ian Reed Radio Drama Prize in 1995 and was produced and broadcast on ABC Radio. Bobis has performed, with dance, excerpts from the third play, *Promenade*, the text of which is one of the long poems in this collection. She has won Philippine national awards for her poetry in both English and Filipino, has completed a collection of short stories, *White Turtle*, and is writing a novel, *Fish-Hair Woman*.

# Summer
# was a Fast Train
# without Terminals

## Merlinda Bobis

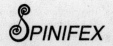

Spinifex Press Pty Ltd
504 Queensberry Street
North Melbourne, Vic. 3051
Australia
women@spinifexpress.com.au
http://www.spinifexpress.com.au/~women

First edition published by Spinifex Press, 1998

Edited by Susan Hawthorne
Typeset in Garamond Light by Claire Warren
Cover design by Deb Snibson, Modern Art Productions
Made and printed in Australia by Australian Print Group


National Library of Australia
Cataloguing-in-Publication data:

CIP
Bobis, Merlinda C. (Merlinda Carullo).
  Summer was a fast train without terminals.
  ISBN 1 875559 76 0
  I. Title.
821

Assisted by Playworks, The Eleanor Dark Foundation Ltd,
and the Centre for Artistic Exchange and Innovation,
University of Wollongong.

## Acknowledgements

*Cantata of the Warrior Woman Daragang Magayon* was first published by the Institute of Women's Studies, St Scholastica's College (Manila, 1993 and 1997).

A number of these poems were originally published in *Rituals*, a collection of the author's poetry (Life Today Publications, Manila, 1990), and in *Southerly, Mattoid, International Feminist Book Fair Journal, Returning a Borrowed Tongue, National Midweek* and *Philippine Studies*.

*Promenade* (performance script, 1995).

## TABLE OF CONTENTS

# WORD GIFTS

*I bring you words freshly
prised loose from my wishbone*

**driving to katoomba**

today, you span the far mountains
with an arm and say,
'this I offer you —
all this blue sweat
of eucalypt.'

then you teach me
how to startle kookaburras
in my throat

and point out orion
among the glow-worms.

i, too, can love you
in my dialect, you know,
punctuated with cicadas
and their eternal afternoons:

'*mahal kita. mahal kita.*'

i can even save you monsoons,
pomelo-scented bucketfuls
to wash your hair with.

and, for want of pearls,
i can string you the whitest seeds
of green papayas

then hope that, wrist to wrist,
we might believe again
the single rhythm passing
between pulses,

even when pearls
become the glazed-white eyes
of a bosnian child
caught in the cross-fire

or when monsoons cannot wash
the trigger-finger clean
in east timor

and when tibetans
wrap their dialect
around them like a robe

lest orion grazes them
from a muzzle.

yes, even when among the sinhalese
the birds mistake the throat
for a tomb

as gunsmoke lifts
from the tamil mountains,

my tongue will still unpetrify
to say,

'*mahal kita. mahal kita.*'

## womansong

sometimes, i think me ready.
i wear the scent of half-mown grass
behind my ears becomingly
and glisten freshly scrubbed by rain.
how my toes curl in tight,
in barefoot quiver,
almost at the brink of cry
digging deeply into earth.

i even travel fringes
of the rose i wear,
the way a finger wonders
at the outline of lips
and its early morning ache.
and then, i hush all growth
in one sharp intake of breath,
when earth is mutely listening for life.

these times, i think me pulled
into acres of strange vegetation,
urged intimate with alien trees;
oh, wrenched away from me
into the greenest country
of the arms of him,
and only him who'd memorise
the pulsing hollow in my throat
enough to speak my woman's tongue.

## prancing

all this grey mist chops off my head,
making it look like a most natural accident.
it rolls off crazy — to the rescue!
i refuse to die today.

so i grab it back to place,
armed with the vengeance
of high noons i blaze about.
i leap into a giant skirt

of one hibiscus on fire,
and swing my flaming flounces
gypsy-like to flaunt myself as red
(shame on the sun).

my arms are banana leaves
unfurling green flags
that wage love against the wind —
i am left raving at its timidity!

today, i am a she-goat kicking aside
the stupidity of fences,
and growing thunders for eyes.
i stare a voice into this tight-lipped day

that can easily swoon
into a night as dumb.
even the pure lilies are not spared —
no, not the lilies, please,

the painfully white hands
of nuns and queens —
i spill my flush all over them,
until their last white speck

is smothered red and deadly.
then we kill
the tameness of the day
twice in a row — i push it further,

my lethalness, and shake all papaya trees
till they chatter to fruiting
and hurl myself deep into the pulp
of one unsuspecting yellow-gold,

lodge there deep like some atom-worm
that can blow its flesh
into a pungent spray of 'what the hell!'
and seeds — sky-high, mind you.

i love too beautifully today
as if tomorrow i will die.
i even tie my hair from cliff to cliff
and invite tightrope dancers.

## siesta

take me not
in mid-winter,
only to thaw the frost
of your old bones,
imagining how stallions rear
in the outback,
hooves raised to this august light,

*kakaibang liwanag,*
*kasimputla't kasinglamig*
*ng hubad na peras.*[1]

but take me
on a humid afternoon
made for siesta,
when my knees almost ache
from daydreaming of mangoes,
tree-ripe
and just right,

*at higit sa lahat*
*mas matamis, makatas*
*kaysa sa unang halik ng mansanas.*[2]

---

1  'alien light,
      as  pale and cold
      as a naked pear'

   plucked from my tongue         you have wrapped
   in a plastic bag with the $3 mango
   from woolworths

   while i conjured an orchard
   from back home — mangoes gold and not for sale, and

2  'above all,
      sweeter, more succulent
      than the first  kiss of the apple.'

# word gifts for an australian critic

i bring you words freshly
prised loose from my wishbone.

*mahal, oyayi, halakhak, lungkot, alaala.*

mate those lips,
then heave a wave in the throat
and lull the tip of the tongue
at the roof of the mouth.
*mahal. mahal. mahal.*
'love, love, love' — let me,
in my tongue.

then i'll sing you a slumber tale.
*oyaiiyaiiyaiiyayiiiii* — once,
mother pushed the hammock
away — *oyaiiyaiiyaiiyayiiiii,*
the birthstrings severed from her wrist
when i married
an australian.

so now i can laugh with you.
*halakhak!* how strange.
your kookaburras roost in my windpipe
when i say, 'laughter!'
as if feathering a new word.
*halakhak-k-k-k-kookaburra!*

but if suddenly you pucker
the lips — *lung* —
as if you were about to break
into tears or song — watch out,
the splinter cuts too far too much — *lungggggggg* —

unless withdrawn — *kot* —
in time. *lungkot*.
such is our word for sadness.

ah! for relief, release, wonder or peace
in any tongue. 'ah!'
of the many timbres;
this is how remembering begins — ah! —
and is repeated — lah!-ah!-lah!
*alaala*. this is our word for memory.

how it forks
like a wishbone.

*mahal, oyayi, halakhak, lungkot, alaala.*

how they flow
east-west-east-west-east
in one bone wishing
it won't break.

## nightwatch from across some highway

your nape
the moon

and you
don't even
know

## border lover

right after my long flight,
i wore it on a tree.
under a canopy of green flags,
my banana heart
magenta velveteen and just
beginning to open.

my petticoated flirt:
three layers of heartskin unfurled
in the air,
*à la* monroe flashing
not pale legs,
but tiny yellow fingers
strung into a filigree of topazes.

but yesterday,
grandmother plucked it,
stripped it to the core,
desecrating aesthetics and romance,
and cut it in two.

one half she served fresh,
dressed in vinegar;
the other, she cooked in coconut milk and chilli
while humming about young girls who fly to learn
strange ideas in a stranger tongue.

later, plying me with more rice,
in the dialect, she said,
'*honi. duwang putahe hale sa sarong puso —*'
here. two dishes from one heart.
i could not eat,
not on a hollow growing
peculiar in my breast.

## stop-over: melbourne airport

this is it.
all the boredom of the world
collected here.

i half-engage their anguish
over the death of a pooch on tv
as the p.a. announces
a two-hour delay.

i pick a pimple.
i let a fingertip
trace maps on my knees.
how sore they are
from too much kneeling at my *mamay*'s wake.

no, black is not for mourning, madam —
so, please don't stare.
i could just be a trendy regular
at darlinghurst cafe.

and these puffy eyes?
just jetlag, sir — look,
i am as bored as all of you;
i have rehearsed this scene enough.
so, there at sydney airport,
when my white man meets me,
no oggling, please.

when i tremble in his arms,
think of it as only a tender scene
reminiscent
of hollywood.

## what he could have written me

at one stop-over,
i folded up my heart
into a crane
for you. a tourist wondered
where i learned *origami*.

then at a street-stall
in the rain,
i asked for *tom-yum*,
two fragrant bowls in all —
the vendor raised her brows
and searched behind my back.

you see, i have arranged
tables for two
in cafes heavy with incense
and chatter
of the most beautiful strangeness
you sometimes have betrayed
in sleep.

once, i dreamt your brown back
was too bare
there at china beach,
I then hunted for you
the whitest of *ao daï*s.

last night,
i tried your number
nine times
between swigs of *basi*
and smoothing pillows —

how come your voice remembered
dawns so much
like this murmur
of fisherfolk
hauling the night's catch?

## reading

your words
are caught
hands.

i move easily
under fingers,
because

your words
are caught
hands.

**in bed with lorca**

when fringe of lips
and tips of hair
run a sweet fever
at one o'clock in the morning

when a shameless nipple
stares like a hot-hard eye
at one o'clock in the morning

when the little finger
and the little toe
burn holes on wind and earth

it is the hour of the gypsy heart
vagrant of my lover's body
cul-de-sac of belly

avenue of thigh
still dark and silent
at one o'clock in the morning

when the whole world sleeps
save me who waits
for the double somersault
of the heart

**print**

each pore brims in brine,
in crystalled sea-pulse,

traps all time,
beating long and slow.

it cannot let go;
just read my back.

i know this skin,
this memory of turtles.

## river

my sarong betrayer re-weaves
its flowers into fishes
that skirt a hipbone
luminous as a stripped banana stalk
and paler than the heart of the palm

## hair ritual

not for the palate this fistful of coconut freshly
grated and this half a green lemon on my other
palm not for a potion either these whitest webs
that could have promised milk for my lover's
curry or this green dome sour enough to make
his tongue invent maledictions against spirits
life is simpler here i'm only off to the river to
wash my hair with coconut and lemon the way
grandmother did before grandfather saw her trail
her hair to her ankles under a moon full of orioles
and giant red and blue dragonflies stories of them
he heard on that fateful night when he saw her
loved her till his deathbed — but i am a twentieth-
century woman and the moon is not full tonight
and orioles and giant dragonflies have gone to
extinction and grandmother now wears her hair
in a grey bob and i am only off to the river with
coconut and lemon to wash my hair for him who
buys shampoos at the chemist — thus moonless
i shall rub white milk and sour juice on my breast-
length strands pretend my fingertips are storytelling
the yellow of orioles the red-blueness of dragonflies
to my scalp tingling as i chant grandmother's name
in the morning he of the chemist wisdom will ask
about winged things of strange colours and why in
the world i wear my hair to my ankles curving like
half-moons and whether he could kiss them too

**going ethnic**

when i met you,
you even wished to learn
how to laugh in my dialect.

between the treble of bees
and the deep bass of water buffalos
on tv's 'world around us'.
between the husk and grain of rice
from an asian shop.
between my palms
joined earnestly
in prayer,

you searched for a timbre
so quaint,
you'd have to train your ears
forever, you said.

and when I told you how we village girls
once burst the moon with giggles,
you piped, 'that must have been
a thrilling sound,
peculiar, ancient
and really cool —

can't you do that again?'

## deck the landscape

'and why wear wattle on your hair
to a barbecue?
we don't do that here,' you said.

strange, i know,
as gringos grilling
on a high noon beach in puerto galera or pattaya.

so leave my hair alone
and all my 'alien aussie-ness'.

have I not '*wok*-en up' your prawns
with sweet chilli?

and gingered your lamb
into *haute cuisine*?

excuse the questions now.
i'm sure, back home,
we're too polite to ask

why a photo-hungry tourist
wears to church
his singlet and his thongs.

## at cafe chic

we have the eyes
of the town

cooling my coffee
and making my cookie fidget
as you piano on my thigh.

we have the eyes
of the town

scanning the ebony-ivory cliche
of our keyed-up skins —
for viruses, perhaps?

could be my un-demure asian-ness
to your aussie slime,

or your slightest paunch
mistaken as extended tumescence.

could be this black coral amulet
nestled on my breast
before my village learned about ecology

or that playboy mag
hot under your cappuccino.

could be anything
that won us
the eyes of the town.

or, perhaps, we could have gotten
the wrong order — is all —
and someone is complaining.

## the vendor

she squats on high noon,
a burnt mascot in her lair —
i swear there is smoke
rising from her nape!

her palm, a dark leaf
on her eyes, moves me,
for where her fingers part,
the sun pulls through with conviction.

her steel squint is what i wish
to buy for its seeming endlessness
upon her mangoes,
so i inch closer — her eyes,

a relief of mist
where we both cool our brows.
oh, we are too shy
to spill this sudden kinship,

so i end up with her warm, warm mangoes.

## in a room to let

every night from work,
she proceeds to test for damp
the lingerie redundant on the line.
the wash are shadows of other hangings;
they need to be tucked away
like virtue nightly slipped
into an old rose vanity.

she shuts her windows tightly
from a fire-wall never higher than her grim
stare, and begins to strip away
the sharp opaqueness of the day.
she resists the sin of a lone mirror;
it might reveal her luminous.

a monotone of rice and fish
is laid out then — the voyeur yellow bulb
is asked to dinner. it's their affair
to have it hug her limbs,
and gentle them to grace.
she squints in welcome
of its savage repetition on her face.

nightcap follows, a glass of milk
for gut-wounds. they nag for feasts
that hush with sleep.
tucked between eight and nine,
the willing mattress holds her down,
its weight unstirring as a mother's arms.
she, too, does not stir,

except on moments when her hands flail,
ever slightly, to toss aside

this mother's clasp
in dreams of maybe younger arms.
but they only flail-flop
back to her breast
like some impotent reliquary.

her mouth half-opened
cups the darkness for posterity.
so she does not hear the rustle,
the young wife's skirt,
the fabric-sigh that ransoms
the next room from shadows.

## mother's break

warmest noons when she feels breathlessly
wedged between sink and bed, she rips off
apron and womb to strike a regal pose
under the infinity of lines of washing.
drenched in midday glow, her colours show
beyond her husband's myth — wife, mother,
whore at times — but she is real now!
stretching back and life in her thin housegown,
which missed its print of roses long ago,
she affirms her non-fictionness
to sunlight. she sniffs, rather airily,
and stamps her foot, perking up her ears
to hear the earth resounding — oh, but
the roast is burning and the youngest
howling above the husband's hungry call!
how well they learn their cues, she sighs,
flushed roses suddenly and hurrying.
aproned with her womb again, she rushes back
to them, to all of them auditioning for love.

## the flower man

he has this hump
from too much bending
levelled only to the shrubs
where he is daily lost.

the spareness of him
hides and hides among
chrysanthemums and roses
which memorise his face.

no five-foot souls
have seen it or the earth
that rims his nails
to stay — only these

smaller creatures know
how funnily he apes
the morning's breath-
lessness as it smothers

their waking cups
with dew or how the quiet
lushness of his stare
loves even stumps to bud.

it is his feeling
almost faint at a loud
profusion he can't take,
which sends a titter

through his charges,
he trowels with his fate.
but a hibiscus-hedge
is promptly hushed —

with a sudden ache,
he reaps the redness
of early roses
for the master's vase.

**penelope unweaving**

there is a time
when we forget the colour
of each others' eyes

and re-invent
old bodysmells
on someone else's thigh.

you with circe and the feast of pigs
or with calypso holding back the sea
from your sheets.

me with a hundred suitors
who need not draw the bow.
they whom I might love at will

and not upon the tedious
whirring of a loom. no, not
from waiting for the rightful groom.

**body parts**

not the womb-curve
of cheek, breast or belly
moves me,

but angles.

i have such reverence
for elbows,
knuckles, knees

bent.

between bone and bone,
griefs freeze,
happy circuits short;

nothing comes full circle.

there, where winter
creeps up on us,
we remember

how human
we are.

## first night

i feed in the train.
she has no english;
her lips round
in a moan
i half-hear, half-imagine, feast upon.
i am greedy for long, drawn-
out vowels.

where her silk sleeves end,
her wrists are blue.
calligraphy of veins
or a word,
a distant hill smudged out?
my tongue recalls
indelible ink.

head bowed,
her little boy clutches his chest
all the way from coledale to central.
i cannot look away.
his knuckles gleam. i think
of pebbles white,
shiny, invading
my mouth.

i push them down
with a gulp of fanta,
but this is my first night in australia.
i can't resist
the train singing,
'a-catch-in-the-throat-
a-catch-in-the-throat —'

## bach at central station

1
some bach
pulls the bow
through my spine.

my bone frets,
remembers threading
the night alone

once in a subway.

2
i am in hot pursuit of his joy
of man's desiring.
it turns a dark corner.

i am a lover tethered
to a fringe of skirt
or to footsteps receeding always
to another alley.

i push ahead,
up the street,
down the next block,

nearly there,
but never quite
catching up.

3
maestro, the music
is in the wrist.

cut it open,
draw out
a skein of notes

that lead me
through the maze
where, anytime,

i will leap at myself,
a minotaur.

## black cat

in its oracular black
it skirts past all
and nothing

i chase it out
over bed, table, chair
through the door

    and lose it

but still i hear a blackness
slithering into shape
whiskers teetering

    between a snarl and grin

as claws are sharpened
against my spine
tightening

    at every prowl

then it stops
waiting as i wait
four eyes lurking in the dark

    it is there

bristling there
within my flailing figure
caterwauling in the night

## panther time

you pantherwoman
        crouched beautiful
you deep black kiss
        that leap
to smother lips
        or wound
with teeth

you stalk me
        wild inside —
i wish you jungled there, caged by trees
        that are my fingers
pushing back, multiplying
        tautly into trunks
as you prowl closer

as you pounce out
        i wish you crushed
against my trees
        but you snarl
daggers
        and trees unfreeze
into fingers again

waiting for the blow —
        you spring —
i grip
        your claw
suddenly turning
        velvet paw

## wargame

brothers knife each other in a game
of soldiers — but they are dry
from father's wounds.
'look, no blood, 'ma!'
their fingers bruise no more,
not even when they pinch the candle at the wick
and lie upon their battle-cots,
while mother moans.

## afternoon madonna

her eyes leap from the crib
to his back being chopped
shorter from her view,
and so she races down,

fast upon the sagging
steps — but his car
revs a noisy relief-ritual
which is a widow's

and the air wears black.
how worn the steps,
she notices at last.
how warped with his descent.

she throws up icy arms
in the afternoon sun;
it chromes her wrists in mid-air,
maybe, to trap and thaw the pulse.

upstairs, it also streams
past wilted diapers — surprise,
the baby makes out angel wings!
his laughter lavishes

itself around and down the steps,
nailing boards in place,
now strong enough to bring
her up. she goes back then,

racing with the hurt,
lest it overtakes her — hardly though;
with this flood of heat,
it simply fizzles out like sweat.

## rita, thirteen

mother glows on my street.
she is beautiful.

can you pick her up?

mother glows on my palm.
she is warm.

can you keep her?

she glows in my pocket.
she is sleeping.

imagine my pocket is full of her,
it glows like a silver cave.

when I slip my hand in,
my fingers turn to silver.

i can buy the world with silver.
i can bribe the world with it.
i can beg the world with it.

to keep all big men away,
because my throat hurts
from too much blowing.

my throat grows a lemon
from too much blowing,
too sour from too much blowing.

## child

i knew you inside.
expelled, you lost a face,
and could get lost
among the bottles in a bio lab.

**daughter dreaming**

when her daughter was dreaming, she planted
a jasmine on the hollow of her back.

when her daughter was dreaming, she dug
with the tip of her fingers and
pushed the petals in.

when her daughter was dreaming, she sang
the tiny flower-tomb shut.

when her daughter was dreaming, she breathed
on a back with no spine — my god,
no bones here, missis.

when her daughter was dreaming, she cried
three hundred and sixty five times
thirteen tears.

when her daughter was dreaming, she fed
on the years of a back forever
curled to the knees.

when her daughter was dreaming, she raged
against the doctor tut-tutting,
a hopeless case, missis — sorry.

so when her daughter was dreaming, she planted
the jasmine and waited till

when her daughter was dreaming, it grew
into a vine where the spine
should have been —

*ay,* vertebrae of flowers uncurling,
unstooping; face lifted for the first time
from this headstone, this damp —

so this is how the sky looks like, mother.
how warm, how sweet.

## detainee

how easily a speck of bird
shatters the evenness of skies —

she peers, stunned, from cell 22

awed that such dumb minuteness
can shake the earth

# PROMENADE

*Summer was a fast train*
*without terminals*

The following performance poem was originally written as a poetry-dance drama for four actors. As a full script, it exists with stage directions and elaborations. Now, pared down to its bare text, I hope the poem can still dance.

# I  Idyll

WOMAN DARK: The white man walks

Out for a walk
with my eyes

WOMAN LIGHT: In gaudy red

WOMAN DARK: Canna-lily red
or ember red
or dream red

WOMAN LIGHT: Tucked into his sillyswagger of pants

WOMAN DARK: Of the most promising tightness

Tight as a throat lodged with song
as a fist of the white shining knuckles

*Ay* what dazzle of hips!

WOMAN LIGHT: But he whitewalks

WOMAN DARK: Out for a walk
with my skin

WOMAN LIGHT: Rough unshaven shoddy

WOMAN DARK: Cacti-chinned    is he?
Grazes the back of my knees
I dream of lichens

WOMAN LIGHT: While his underarms splotch darkly

WOMAN DARK: With continents
for me to walk on
my palms and soles

braille-ing away
his alphabet of pores

MAN LIGHT:     How she walks

MAN DARK:      She darkly walks

MAN LIGHT:     The curve of her calves
               electric!

MAN DARK:      Beware the current of her black belly

MAN LIGHT:     That tightens and rounds
               and tightens    with ease
               this half-cheek of the moon

MAN DARK:      How very brief her skirt

MAN LIGHT:     *Ay* my abbreviated afternoon!

WOMAN DARK:    This devilbrow
               is a cheek's throw
               from my lipglow
               and the nippleknowing
               wisdom

               O sing me a fever
               a fulldraught flush
               a onceuponquiver
               I must not forget
               how it was!

MAN LIGHT:     But I remember
               summer as a fast train
               without terminals

               My sweat careening
               towards my navel's pool

48

I came    drenched derailed

O how I came

from the hotsprings of Rotorua
to the sanddunes of Sahara
On a tomtomnight

I came

radiantly bare-bellied
and shimmying
from humid siestas in Madrid

as I came

thawing out a fiesta
even through the bluest iceberg
of the Arctic

because I came

from the rock    the reddest heart
burgeoning with songlines

O yes I came

just when by an old pagoda
a peach orchard had multiplied
the sun!

WOMAN DARK:    Sun

that made me come

through the fattest eye
of a ricegrain
and the soulandblues of jacaranda

O I came

spangled with Stars of David
on my shoulder curving

like the Nile

I came

as a sharp retort of castanets
to the heady shattering of plates
con-ning me to bella-samba
all the way to Rome

where I came

out     more stately than the Eiffel!

## II    To War

MAN LIGHT:     Summer was a fast train
               without terminals

               My sweat careening
               towards my navel's pool

               I came     drenched derailed

WOMAN DARK:    We did out-come the end
               Did we not?

               Past Troy     Past Jericho  Past Babylon

MAN LIGHT:     Summer was a fast train
               Past France Past Korea Past Vietnam —

WOMAN DARK:    We did out-come the end
               Did we not?

MAN LIGHT      Past ChinaPast NicaraguaPast
               Philippines
               My sweat careening
               I came —

WOMAN DARK:    We did out-come the end
               Did we not?

WOMAN DARK     PastBosniaPastTibetPastRwanda
& MAN LIGHT:   O could we not?

WOMAN LIGHT:   Not not
               ask me not
               about oil and water whoring
               in the riverskin

               Ecological suicide
               is mortal sin

Not not
let not
the dark merge with the light

Preserve *differance*
and ban this dance

Not not
lift not
your skirt
to the pig of a man

Dis-remember his calls
dismember his balls

Not not
ask me not
about oil and water whoring
in the riverskin

Ecological suicide
is mortal sin

WOMAN DARK:    But you are me

under my dark palm

Heart of a white cheek
white lip
white neck
white breast
white hip

is dark

MAN LIGHT:    Red

under my palm pale
cupped
to the curve

of your pulse darkly

tuned
to my wrist
transluscent with light

WOMAN DARK:  Prism'd
by a rainbow

as if after
a surprise sun-
shower

MAN LIGHT:  Blurring
this difference

ofsexofskin

Each one
rained on

WOMAN DARK:  Each one
receiving a blessing

WOMAN LIGHT:  But beware —

this bane
this sacrilege
of the pure colours

MAN LIGHT:  This myth
of the sacrilege
of the pure

Under my palm —

WOMAN DARK:  It breaks!

Like rain
bearing a blessing

MAN DARK:    Bless this ring a ring of roses
a pocket damned with losers
One two three
they both tumbled down

O give me a tumble    she pleaded
Even a toss  he conceded

But black over white
and white over black
will only grey-coat the eye

O toss me a chessboard instead
the blacks and whites distinct
and tumble not Man
but tumble her down

when she begs for the glint
in your eye

WOMAN LIGHT:  A ring a ring of roses
a pocket damned with losers
One two three
they both tumbled down

O steal back the dark
dusk on this pale male

and the white
light in her olive gaze

for colours cavorting
in this frenzied ball

is hardly correct at all

MAN DARK:    Hardly correct

Hardly correct

Hardly correct

Hardly

Hardly

Hardly

WOMAN DARK:    Hard!

O the first harvest of nuts
acorns almonds macadamias
between my teeth

Hard

as a lemon pit
resolving into pearl

Hard

as a grain
worrying my back

as you lay me
lay me

MAN LIGHT:    Hard!

O limber through the eye
of a needle
and see how

Hard

to out-come
the precisioned rhythm
of their thought-out tongue

Hard

as frozen meat!

WOMAN LIGHT:    You dare

thaw the pure palate

MAN DARK: With the blackwhite breath —

WOMAN LIGHT: Hang it!

MAN DARK: Shred it
in the guillotine!

WOMAN DARK  Bitch!
& MAN LIGHT: Pig!

WOMAN LIGHT: You call me that
& MAN DARK

unrepeatable
unspeakable
abominable

name?

WOMAN LIGHT: Get me some chilli
to punish
his sordid tongue

MAN DARK: Or some jasmine brew
to sweeten her breath again

WOMAN LIGHT: And needle and thread
to stitch their lips with!

Cross-stitch, chain-stitch
embroidering their mouths

MAN DARK: Now cripple the tongues!

WOMAN LIGHT: No more speaking
No more kissing

| | |
|---|---|
| MAN DARK: | Then geld the eyes! |
| WOMAN LIGHT: | Sunless, moonless<br>will they be |
| MAN DARK: | And let us open<br>the fanfare! |
| WOMAN LIGHT: | Crime? |
| MAN DARK: | Rooting a white pig<br><br>Crime? |
| WOMAN LIGHT: | Balling a black bitch |
| WOMAN LIGHT:<br>& MAN DARK: | Did you call me    did you say<br>did you<br>Wash your mouth out!<br><br>And let us begin<br>the trial of the blackwhite breath — |
| MAN DARK: | Culture? |
| WOMAN LIGHT: | Female<br>Black<br>From the other side of the river<br><br>Culture? |
| MAN DARK: | Male<br>White<br>From the other side of the mountain |
| WOMAN LIGHT: | Crime? |
| MAN DARK: | Theycame'nsang'ndancedtogether |

| | |
|---|---|
| WOMAN LIGHT: | Verdict |
| | Guilty by a million years |
| MAN DARK: | Sentence |
| | General cleaning of the mouth<br>Sealing off the sex |
| | Self-flagellation |
| | Now let's get on with it |
| WOMAN LIGHT: | Say 'Ah' |
| MAN DARK: | Ah — Ah? |
| WOMAN LIGHT: | Aha! |
| | The cavern the cavern<br>has a naughty spring |
| | The cavern the cavern<br>must be a responsible thing |
| | Repeat after me |
| MAN DARK: | Say 'Ah' |
| WOMAN LIGHT: | Ah — Ah? |
| MAN DARK: | Aha! |
| | The cavern the cavern<br>is a dangerous fool |
| | The cavern the cavern<br>must be a sterilised tool |
| | Sing with me |

WOMAN DARK:   Once a family
              from the other side of the river sang

              Let us dance O let us dance
              the river dance alone
              us alone

MAN LIGHT:    Once a family
              from the other side of the mountain
              sang

              Let us dance O let us dance
              the mountain dance alone
              us alone

MAN DARK      Them mountain folk
              cannot dance with us

WOMAN LIGHT:  Them river folk
              cannot dance with us

WOMAN DARK:   Them folk
& MAN LIGHT:  cannot dance cannot dance

              They have two left feet
              two left feet
              two left feet
              because toes won't burst
              into jungle flowers

              *Ayayayayayyyy!*

              Left-footed dancer
              is dancing out

              a Troy a Babylon
              dancing out
              a European Front
              dancing out
              Korea and Vietnam

dancing out
the Nicaraguan cry

dancing out
a Filipino coup
dancing out
in Bosnia Belfast too

dancing out
Somalian feet
dancing out
the Chechnyan beat
dancing out
the Burmese heat

Yes dancing out
Tibet Rwanda

to the edge
of a bludgeoned sky

*Ayayayayayyyy!*

Left-footed dancer
is dancing out

and toes won't burst
into jungle flowers!

### III Return

MAN LIGHT:    Coming home

I have rehearsed this
a thousand times

in my eyes
my heart
my hands
my knees
my feet

WOMAN DARK:    My tired soldier's

eyes on my mouth
heart on my heart

hands on my hips
knees on my knees

and both our feet
in that silentest conversation

as we dance
as if we've never danced
before

MAN LIGHT:    Never danced before
because I am from the other side
of the mountain

WOMAN DARK:    How your waist spans
like a mountain tree

How it could have rested
on the crook of my arm

But we have never danced before
Because I am from the other side
of the river

MAN LIGHT:    How your waist repeats
              the arc of a ripple

              How my arm longs
              to curve with the current

              But listen —
              a half-dance blooms     at the edge
              of the wail-trail

              Steps of no consequence
              Gyrations betrayed     at the hips
              Fingers clicking  dead

              to the tune of
              *Aaaayyyyyyyyyyyyyyyyyyyyyyyyyyyyyyyyy!*


WOMAN DARK:   Lover Lover
              what is that new dance music
              all about?


MAN LIGHT:    It is about the road to Ithaca
              as far and empty as the eye can reach
              as the song can reach


WOMAN DARK:   And who is playing that song?


MAN LIGHT:    Only no one my dear
              Only no one


WOMAN DARK:   But someone must play
              because someone must dance


MAN LIGHT:    Perhaps it is the wind
              or our wish for a wind
              playing it


WOMAN DARK:   And for whom does a wish play?


62

| MAN LIGHT: | For a left-footed dancer<br>who forgot |
|---|---|
| | that toes can burst<br>into jungle flowers |
| WOMAN DARK: | Let him remember then<br>Let him |
| MAN LIGHT: | I remember summer<br>as a fast train<br>without terminals |
| | My sweat careening<br>towards — |
| | Dachau! |
| WOMAN DARK: | Lover Lover<br>you've lost your lines |
| | No not towards Dachau |
| | It is your sweat careening<br>towards your navel's pool |
| MAN LIGHT: | And I came?<br>Drenched    derailed? |
| WOMAN DARK: | O yes<br>you came<br>from the hotsprings of Rotorua |
| MAN LIGHT: | To the longest winter in Russia<br>To the gravetrail of Kokoda<br>To the bloodstreets of Hiroshima<br>Through the belly of Nanjing |
| | How I came |

Out of a ribcage a rat
out of a limb a fat
worm watching this eye turn
inside out

WOMAN DARK: But then
you came out clean
hounding the breath of strangers
through a wall in Berlin

MAN LIGHT: This hangman's breath
on a child's skin
tight as a drum

in the arms
of a Kurdish mother

WOMAN DARK: But did she not say
play it
beat me a rhythm there
something akin to my baby's pulse

MAN LIGHT: Betrayed by the Timorese air?

WOMAN DARK: But did she not say
perhaps upon this Gaza strip
my son would find

my kiss
an amulet to seal
the lips of his gun

MAN LIGHT: That also seals old wounds?

*Ay* how to stitch
the seams of history?

WOMAN DARK: But can we not say
perhaps on a tomtomnight

we will come through

on nimble feet
without memory

MAN LIGHT:     From a long road to Zaire?

WOMAN DARK:   No!     Never

How without memory
when we both came
from that rock     the reddest heart

burgeoning with songlines

O how we came

just when by an old pagoda
a peach orchard had multiplied the sun!

MAN LIGHT:     Sun
that can never make me come again

through the fattest eye
of a ricegrain

Or the soulandblues of jacaranda

Never again

to be spangled
with Stars of David

on my shoulder curving
like the Nile

Never

as a sharp retort of castanets

Never

to be rescued

by the shattering of plates

Never bella
Never samba

Never coming-dancing out

more stately than the Eiffel!

WOMAN DARK: Hush Lover hush

MAN LIGHT: We could not out-come
out-dance the end

Could we?

WOMAN DARK: Hush Soldier hush

MAN LIGHT: But play me a wish anyhow
Dance me a wish

WOMAN DARK: Hush Dancer hush

It is deep night now
at the other side of the river
at the other side of the mountain

lost in a swoon
of bones

MAN LIGHT: And the sky
O the sky

is my dark footprints
gathered always

by the scythe
of a moon

# CANTATA OF THE WARRIOR WOMAN DARAGANG MAGAYON

*What wisdom in tradition*
*that can kill*

According to a Philippine myth, Mount Mayon, an active volcano in the Bikol region of southern Luzon, is the tomb of Princess Daragang Magayon (Beautiful Maiden). Against her will, she marries the belligerent warlord Datu Pagtuga in order to save her father and tribe from war. During the wedding, her lover Prince Ulap attempts to rescue her. He kills Pagtuga, but Linog, Pagtuga's henchman, slays Ulap. The princess dies during the encounter. Her tomb grows into Mayon volcano, whose name derives from her own, Magayon.

The following poem radically departs from the myth. In this re-made telling, the volcano does not simply rise from the tomb of Magayon. Instead, this mountain of fire is seen as 'the ascent of rage/and grief of a whole tribe' during a war.

This poem was shaped in two languages, Filipino and English; the writing involved a constant struggle between them. The final version now exists in each language.

**PROLOGUE**

*To the Mountain*

Daragang Magayon,
in this half-light, you stun me.
You repeat a crestpeak
breaking against the sky;
a once-upheaval caught
at its height — against the clouds,
a breast heaved and held
with no letting go of breath,
that swell of fury from all ages.

*Ay,* you stretch this eye
to the peak of the mind,
as you would pull visions
sky-high and almost blind
with too much wind.
You strain me to be bird
this early morning,
I almost hear me
growing wings.

Down here,
your immense sweep
of bluish-grey-green
becomes briefest in my wonder.

Thousands of feet I fly
in a handspan,
in one sharp intake of breath
when everything is fast yet still.

I shall know you earth
more than mountain-fire.
That bluish-grey-green shall loom
a deeper shade, shaping tree,
leaf, grass and dew on its tip.
I shall know you
in that firmest breast
stunning me to a flash of wing.

The day moves
and you are capped with clouds
I firmly elbow out.
I am jealous —
I wish you brightest,
clearest, as personal
as a lump in the throat
full as this morning.

Is this how to choke
in too much beauty
that splinters the eye?
You stun me bird
in its first leap of wing.
You lift me to that peak,
a spreading sense of earthlessness
with too much earth.

Like knowing my name
for the first time.

I soar and yearn
for airless closeness
where I could tell you to my body
again and again,
and you could tell me back
as fire. *Ay,* this smouldering of eyes,
this acheful kindling of the thighs
as I begin to fold my wings
quivering to roost.

But is this the peak,
this strangest crest,
this hideous breast?
Up close, so like one hacked
by the madness of winds.
You stun me more
with deep ravines that gash,
with cliffs that bruise
and roughest grooves.

Where is the slope that heaved
and nippled to the sun,
that perfect wave which knew
no flaw, no lack?
Something vicious
about a wounded mountain,
a breast that suckled monster teeth.
Your name unclasps from memory.
I do not know you
ravaged to the foot.

I can not love you
with no name.

## Reply of the Mountain

Lovers are better nameless.
It is enough to suckle sky
and wing the eye.
My lover has to see
beyond a breast or crest.
He has to know
my deepest grooves.
I have to wound his eye
beyond desire.

So I am the volcano,
a breast holding up the sky
and billowing a skirt;
at my foot, the earth,
unending lawn for all feet.
But I am only beautiful
for those below
who have been stunned sky-high,
all chance-birds waiting
for first time flights,
all of you.

Up here, you cannot know me
as fullest crest of earth,
as roost for all fliers,
rest for tired wings.
You deny me —
because I am wounded?
Come, let me bruise you
with my broken flesh.
I have not promised
tenderness alone.

Gather all my grooves
that cut the pupil.
Do not blink;
do not shrink
from the tremor of lids.
My deep ravines are not far
from the reddish furrows
running the whiteness of your eyes.

Know me now
in the years you dreamt,
the tossing of days
that desired to rise
in the hit-beat of each minute
that deepened grooves into gashes,
into wounds not mine alone,
these pangs of need to limn
our different grasping
for air or earth or fire.

How distant then our hands.
Apart, we used to curl these fingers
around a possibility of touch,
but clutched alone the shock,
the always baldness of our palms.
But we eased the fist
and made a clearing between fingers,
enough to weave in other fingers —
to make a cup for kindred stirrings

that we caught while touching,
and could not spill.
Do you remember?
They live in tales
we always bring to life together

when we desire in flesh,
and then desire beyond desire.
Do you remember?
There was a song we sang
again and again —

Flight is song
on four winds.
From the east,
a voice blows ripe
and ricegrain-gold.
From the west,
another teems
with silver fish.

Flight is song
on four winds.
From the north,
a voice rushes
in pollen-breath.
From the south,
another hums
the glint of stars.

Flight is song
on four winds.
Day to night,
gold is minted
into silverfin;
dark to light,
stars will seed
to pollenbright.

Flight is song
on four winds.

Earth and sea
and air and sky
blow and teem
and rush and hum
into the dreaming
of a single weave.

This is the limning song,
the healing song that spurs
all separate hands to clasp
and knit the cleaved skin.
Remember this song.
Tomorrow, I will unravel
its weave. I will tell you
the tale of each strand,
even the tales before it

to make known what is known,
but kept as unknown, in song.
I will sing us again and again
till we are levelled
by the passing wind,
so that in such time of plains,
when we lie as one flat stillness,
no one shall wonder
why together we sleep
in a conspiracy of dreams
of those that we tell
and those that we keep.

*To the Mountain*

Not a story, but a name
is what I need.
How do I know you
without a name?
What name is no name?

Peel the grooves
from my eyes.
I wish to see Daragang Magayon,
and believe. Woman,
bring the brightness back,

the fullest breast,
the smoothest sweep of earth,
the bluish grey and green.
Gift back this eye
its power to define

as you have gifted wings.
You named me as a bird
believing in mountains,
so I flew to know the peak
and speak the name

of one who named.
You never promised wounds
that scar the eye.
You never promised
this shattering of flight.

## Tale of the Mountain

Once they called me Daragang Magayon,
a name that means Beautiful Maiden.
A curse lurked in that name.
I was hair, eyes, lips,
breasts and feet of fire.
I was holy. I was religion.
Maiden-bound, I was desired;
bold hunter's bounty,
game and fruit trembling close
to seeking lips and teeth
that sink to tame.
I was. I was a name.

Daragang Magayon.
Beautiful Maiden.

A name that cringes at blood?
But I bleed when the moon rounds,
a heart-womb flow
that shatters gods.
I refused Pagtuga, the hunter
who bound my father
and waged war against our kingdom,
so he could take my flesh.

You think I blush at flesh?
I kiss the skin
of sky, water, land;
I quiver boldly
at a brush with hands.
*Ay,* my lover and his limbs,
his rousing vine
that makes me burst into mangoes
and guavas ripening at touch.

But I am more than fruit
that feeds the eye or mouth.
Have you known me
beyond skin, beyond name?
You heard the wrong story.
You should have caught
rumours, those that we whisper
and those that we keep,
the beat of the pulse,
the cry in one's sleep.

So let me shape the cry,
a dagger to your calm,
a blade sharpened upon your ear.
Let me tell you my story
of unnaming. I stripped me
of my precious name.
I killed Daragang Magayon.
I am now The Nameless One.
*Ako Ang Warang Pangaran*
*Na Kagsadiri Kang Gabos Na Pangaran*.
I am The Nameless One Who Is All Names.

# I    BAKONAWA

DARAGANG MAGAYON:  No one sleeps tonight.
The dark insists
our palmwings stay open
and beat in the weave
of nightsounds
to shatter the drowsy still
in each quiver.
*Ay,* the answer of shard,
the sting in the pupil.

Do not sleep tonight.
Brave a wakeful eye
and see —
the air wears black,
because the moon was swallowed
by that monster in the sky,
the glutton Bakonawa.
Swollen with the moon,
with our womb
that gives birth to the sun.

Look, his dragon-body
curls in sleep,
and how he snores,
sated with his feast.
That grin is fixed.
He must be dreaming
of more moons to eat,
moons full and pregnant

with the sun.
How his darkness looms,
but we never sleep.

This is Rawis, our kingdom.
No moon,
but unscarce in light.
It is a thousand pairs of moon,
the white of staring eyes.
It is a thousand crowd of fires,
the mind alive.
Do not sleep tonight;
to sleep is to die.

Remember, tomorrow is the battle
with the spurned Pagtuga,
that other Bakonawa who prowls
not the sky but the earth.
He comes to feed on me
and on the flesh of our tribe.
I can hear him heave;
the enemy is near.

So we must dig out the moon
from the belly of his blood-brother,
that glutted dragon in the sky.
We need the moon
to birth the sun.
In the light of mind and eye,
sharpen the blade,
and cut the gut,
kill the monster,
bear the sun!

And listen carefully.
There is a trapped throb
in the fire of our hands;
from heart
to fingertips,

this burst of life.
It seems like palmwing
lifting, becoming sole
treading the sky.

We shall set it free.
More than throb,
it will be drums — drums!
Did we not let fly then
the beat of rage?
Did we not stir the nightwind mad?
Listen to that old ritual once again.
There was a time
when we kept the beast at bay.

WOMEN:    *Ayyyyy*, Bakonawa,
          the moon is not your feast.
          *Ayyyyy*, Bakonawa,
          We curse your gut to shrinking!

DARAGANG MAGAYON:    Many full moons ago,
                     the women sang and danced
                     in rhythm with their bodies.
                     From tenderness to frenzy,
                     voices and arms and feet
                     spun the dark to light.

WOMEN:    My womb is the moon,
          the weaver of shades
          in the darkest of night
          of the bone and the flesh.

          And the moon ripens,
          deepening into sun,
          into a wide-eyed morning,
          keeper of life.

SIRANGAN:    Moonsong and lightdance.
             The caress of the sole

is a stroke on the moon.
The embrace of the voice
has the sun in embrace.

Come, Daragang Magayon,
this is the *Halya*,
our ritual-battle
against Bakonawa.

Moonsong and lightdance.
Poetry to fight
the glutton monster.

Come, Daragang Magayon,
the rite has begun.
Come, we will guard the full moon
and wait for it
to bear the sun.

DARAGANG MAGAYON: My nurse, my dear Sirangan calls,
a voice that breaks
but never roughly,
not like glass.
I could easily close my hands
around it as it croons,
'Hush, *padaba, padaba* —'
beloved, beloved.
Sirangan, I hear you again
in the wind of that past,
as if its skein of years
were untwining old songs.

*Ay,* your lullabies, Sirangan,
for this child who did not know
   a mother
except for a name
that you sang at my cot
moons and moons ago.
'Dawani. Dawani. Dawani —

on a night when the moon
was full and sleepless,
she bore you,
and slept and slept.'

Did you sing to her, too,
when you came to nurse her?
Did you also call her '*padaba*'?
Dawani never died
in your heart, Sirangan.
Again and again, you kissed
her name on my lips,
like blood-giving.
Sirangan, my nurse,
my mother, were you alive
in this moonless night,
you would kiss me the sun.

So many moons ago
since you stroked my hair
and tamed with song
the darkness in my sleep;
so many moons ago
since mothers and fathers
sang to their babies
not to fear. Now they sing
to soothe themselves,
but not for rest,
because the moon has died;
it is pitch-dark
in their old nightstare.

I had just turned twelve
when you took me to the women
for the first time.
They wondered why the daughter
of Datu Makusog should dance
with them, my father's slaves.
Master dancing with her subjects?

Heaven and earth weaving
     their feet
and sharing one breath?

I thought, how dark the skin
of most of them — like night.
Darker than yours, Sirangan.
I wished to ask,
are these the people
from the far mountains of eagles
that soar in your songs?
Should I dance with them?
Is it right? You pushed me gently
towards them.

Me in my silken clothes
smelling of cedar chests,
and vain in my heavy gold.
And these feet,
tentative yet ready,
mincing on my biting thoughts
about their skin-colour,
with only half a heart
desiring dance, dance, dance!

Its other half was wondering —
with them? With dark hands
     and feet
that dug my father's fields
and fished for him?
But how they danced
in their wild flowers and shells,
their wave of earthsea passion,
cresting smell of sun and salt
and freedom — I was as stiff
as a petrified branch.

But something loosed my hair
from its pearl-twined knot

and winged my limbs
as our voices brimmed
and our pulses throbbed
in a common dance.
Somewhere in our wombs,
we knew each other not by name.
We knew not skin, but sweat.

And they loved the drums
with their palms — beating, beating!
The bells were rung
to the pulse of our feet
as we sang to scare Bakonawa.
He could not eat the moon.
He fled with his army of beasts,
and Yasaw, his minister of shadows,
slithered back to the deep forest.

But that was moons ago.
Now, Yasaw hisses in our midst,
scales rippling in wild elation,
because Bakonawa has fed well.
So we will dance again
and ransom the moon from his gut.
We will birth the sun
for the greater battle tomorrow.

Remember, there is another
    Bakonawa.
He is not of the sky,
he who comes to feed
on me and our people.
He is Pagtuga, Datu of the tribe
    of Isarog.
Pagtuga, the spurned hunter.
Pagtuga drooling for a younger
    womb;
twice, he nearly raped me
before he murdered my old nurse.

Then he hunted my father,
his wild boar, and held him
in his kingdom, then threatened us
with war — to bind my will?
To barter my blood
for my blood? *Ayyy*, I will dance
on his grave! In the light
of mind and eye,
I sharpen my blade
and dance on his grave —

I carve this air
with my body swaying
to the drums in my breast.

The back of my hand
curves on my palm,
one dance, one life.

My every turn
vanquishes old curve
and line of lust.

I free this form
marked with desire alone,
I wing this body from its mould.

I am more than body.
I am heart. I am mind.
I am mine. I am mine.

How delicious is the rhythm
when a turn is the turn of the mind
that answers the drums in the breast,

the gods of my heart,
these spirits chanting back,
chanting back the light
that shall stain in crimson.

Dawani, beat the earth!
Sirangan, beat the sky!
My mothers who are my gods,
dance with me!

Whip the wind
into fury with hair
undone and flying,

like a thousand crows
whose blackest cries
unstill the soul.

No one rests tonight.
Even the leaves
must burn like eyes.

Never forget
their black-green fire
that kept vigil
with the rest of us
who stamped the earth,
as if our soles
would make it shriek as well.
How we danced and raged
against Bakonawa.

SIRANGAN:          Watch her dance.
Twelve years old with wrists
     of green,
palest ricesprouts hinting
seeds of the sun.
A pulse just rousing.
What morning will rise on her palm?
What palm will carve out fire
from these fields?

WOMEN:          What a beautiful child!
Why bring her here, Sirangan?

The Princess can not dance
   with slaves.

SIRANGAN:            Let her round
as human beings need to wax
like moons to fullness.
No crescent, no half-moon,
no half-woman will she be.
We have no need
for unripened visions.

WOMEN:              What if her father knows?
Why tarnish gold
with loam?
His gold of all gold,
his dearest child
from the late Dawani.

SIRANGAN:            The hand weighs the fistful sheen
and clutches it. It is not tender,
nor does it love, this grip that owns
the gold — our Datu is wiser
than we think.
His child is a child,
and not a coffered thing.

DARAGANG MAGAYON: A woman is not a wild boar
chased by the hunter,
not a prized head that fires
his limp shaft brave
and swollen-dumb —
this inescapable shaft of kings?
Pagtuga, we are ready
for the battle tomorrow.
You have wounded us
even before the first wound.
How our rage spills red
as a sky on fire,
even before it burns.

But moons ago,
my twelve-year-old eyes
burned with another crimson
in that ritual-dance.

YOUNG DARAGANG
MAGAYON:

My skirt has a red wound, Sirangan,
and fire runs between my legs.
The ire of the gods
is on me — because I danced
with slaves? This blood,
this gushing heat,
this curse on a princess
that carved the wind
with her slaves.
They say it should not be,
our rhythms should not weave
into one pattern of the wind.

SIRANGAN:

Your daggertongue breaks
the closest flesh.
How innocence can cut.
*Padaba*, this is the nurse
you love, serving in your father's
    house.
These dark slave-arms
that rocked you as a baby
did not bruise your flesh.
The lullabies that stilled
the shadows of your dreams
did not blight your wind.
It is a dagger, Daragang Magayon,
your tongue that deepens
the cut, the brand of slaves.

YOUNG DARAGANG
MAGAYON:

But Father said
you are different.
I do not see your meaning.
I am bleeding, Sirangan.
I am afraid.

| SIRANGAN: | What is the balm for blindness? |
|---|---|

| YOUNG DARAGANG MAGAYON: | I am afraid. |
|---|---|

| SIRANGAN: | How to see the only colour of wombs. |
|---|---|

DARAGANG MAGAYON:  I am afraid. I do not deny
this tightening in my breast.
But this is not my twelve-year-old
    fear,
not any more. Not that shuddering
at the rush of red from my sex
which I did not understand.
Not the fear of the blind
who groped for a curse
to explain her blood
upon dancing with slaves.

Tonight is different;
mine is the warrior's fear.
Before each battle,
a beast squats on the lid
of the squinting eye,
more foe than the foe.
It creeps to the pupil,
dives deep to the breast
to seize the heart
or be seized by the heart.
*Ay,* the blood!

Sirangan, I need you now
to slay this beast
nesting in my eye
the way you crushed
its older kin when I was twelve.
That other beast,
a monstrous splinter,

saw our people then
only as shade of their skin.

Only as headgears whose colours
brand them master, freefolk or slave.
How a coil of cloth about the skull
can wind around the mind
and even overwhelm the eyes.
Blindness and fear;
fear and blindness,
what closest kin.

I remember well
my ritual-dance
on unseeing eyes.
The splinter there
must have urged the white
to swallow the black.
Even the irises were not spared.

YOUNG DARAGANG    The wound on my skirt —
MAGAYON:    it is very red, Sirangan.

SIRANGAN:    Do not fear, *padaba.*
It is the first blood
from the womb, a cleansing ritual
with the rounding of the moon,
and not the ire of gods
who cursed your dancing
with slaves.
Daragang Magayon,
there is no curse.

With this ripening of womb,
could we not ripen in the mind
to clear the eye
and see a single world
between earth and sky?
The right to be human

is born with everyone as bones
lending shape to flesh.
This is no boon bestowed
by the branding eye.

Red is the only colour
of all wombs.
Red is the only colour
of all blood
under different skins.
There is a beast in your eye,
my child, an ugly splinter.

WOMEN:                    *Hala!* Let us feast
                         after the ritual of the *Halya*.
                         We have scared Bakonawa.

FIRST WOMAN:             Serve the princess first.

SECOND WOMAN:            *Hoy*, taste not her food
                         lest you be punished.
                         Beware, your stomach shall
                         ache and swell like the gut
                         of a toadfish. Remember the Elders'
                         story about the curse
                         against any slave who eats
                         from the master's plate.

FIRST WOMAN:             I wonder how true.

SECOND WOMAN:            It is best to be cautious.

WOMEN:                   Serve the princess!

                         And let us drink.

                         Let the *tigsik* begin.

FIRST WOMAN:             I toast to this glass,

|  |  |
|---|---|
|  | count to three<br>and I will drain it fast. |
| SECOND WOMAN: | Be sure you gulp it down.<br>All of it — |
| FIRST WOMAN: | Finished!<br>See, the glass is drained.<br>Now, anybody, answer my toast. |
| SECOND WOMAN: | I toast to Bakonawa.<br>We think he is of giant frame,<br>yet he lodges there,<br>a splinter in our eye. |
| FIRST WOMAN: | Hoy, why toast to the monster?<br>And how could you think<br>he is but dirt in the eye?<br>All beasts are larger than the eye;<br>Bakonawa is larger than we are.<br>How could a splinter eat the moon? |
| SECOND WOMAN: | A splinter blinds us to the moon,<br>blinds us to the light. |
| FIRST WOMAN: | How could a splinter eat the moon? |
| WOMEN: | Enough! Let us get on with the<br>          *tigsik.* |
|  | Yes! Yes! |
|  | The *tigsik!* The toast! |
| DARAGANG MAGAYON: | I toast to all humanity.<br>Small and big, the same worth.<br>Big and small, the same use.<br>This was their *tigsik* before.<br>This is still our toast today. |

Pagtuga, our measure
is not in strength,
and our right is not in gold,
pearls, or heads of the hunt
which you heaped at my feet
to bind them to your will.

In the years after that dance
in the ritual of the *Halya*,
I saw how all hands
of different colours
push the earth to turn.
One hand could bind all hands,
but the world spins on —
the pulse unknots the fear.
This drum beats,
breaks, burns the cord.

WOMEN:          You think it was right?

She danced with us.

How fast she learned our steps.

*Ay,* how beautiful!

First burst of the earth
and ricesprouts' kin;

our eyes, our eyes,
they shimmer green
with your moonlit skin.

Daragang Magayon,
Our Beautiful Maiden.

Daragang Magayon.
Daragang Magayon.
Daragang Magayon.

DARAGANG MAGAYON:  During that dance,

they also named me with their eyes.
Also a baptism of slaves,
that branding of my form.
But it did not sting,
the wound I took with pride.
There was no bracing of the skin.

But now I know how deep the gash,
now that Pagtuga names me
in his name with eyes that sear
the marrow. I can smell it
burning under his heat.

*Ay*, Pagtuga, do not be too sure
about the battlefield.
Tomorrow, I will also rend that gaze
in a dagger-dance.
This blade of my body
will cut the beast,
the lurking splinter
in your marking stare.

## II MAGAYON

DARAGANG MAGAYON: They chose a name that silenced me.
My lips forgot to grow
their private syllables;
I was too busy chanting older gods.
How I loved their eyes,
the soft, soft 'yes'
that gathered me,
beautiful beloved of their tribe.
It was so easy to be dumb
and dance the figures in their gaze.

Listen here to my baptism.
They called the names of the dead
to seal my life.

MIDWIFE: Banutaw.
Wara-wara.
Nanoma.
Mutya.
Bulan-bulan.

WOMEN: Chant them loud and clear,
the names of all her ancestors.
Her wailing has to stop;
the name that stills her cry
shall be her chosen name.

DARAGANG MAGAYON: How easy then to succumb

to the cosy little room
that makes a given name;
the space is cleared and cut
for you. You can grow
without wondering how far.
*Ay,* only to that other end,
that final letter
crouched against the wall.

WOMEN:                    It is a good name, is it not?
                         Daragang Magayon meaning
                         Beautiful Maiden. What delicious
                         rhythm on the tongue.
                         So right for a girl, Sirangan.
                         The Datu will be pleased.

SIRANGAN:                I would rather she were named
                         from rivers or seas, or even rain.
                         It is good to be water
                         without shape,
                         conjuring many faces.

DARAGANG MAGAYON:  Now I would rather be water
                         but unnamed, Sirangan.
                         Being and breaking and being,
                         all my fluid shards
                         all private syllables
                         that link themselves at will
                         into shape, then burst apart again
                         into shapelessness.

                         It is our cycle of blood
                         we endlessly round like moons
                         and shatter into rivers.
                         We are self-spun
                         in our waterlooms,
                         bodies weaving 'once upon a time'
                         and 'now', refusing to be told

how and when or where to flow.
I would rather be water
and unnamed.

But, as a child, I mouthed stories
they told of my body.
It had a form, a finished weave,
a tautness in its warp and weft
that could not breathe.

MIDWIFE:

Let us finish the ritual.
The beauty rite this time,
the shaping of her head.
A heavy piece of wood on the brow
and another pressed
against the back of the head
to flatten the skull — there.

SIRANGAN:

Pity the newborn. The pressing
    wood
will break her skull.

MIDWIFE:

This shall be done with utmost care.

SIRANGAN:

Hear her wailing.
*Ay,* spare the infant.
Must we mould her head?
The sculpting palms
are most dangerous.

WOMEN:

This has been done before.
It must be done again today
and tomorrow. Rituals repeat
themselves as in chanting.
Never a break between.

SIRANGAN:

What wisdom in tradition
that can kill.

In the tribe where I was born,
we had no such ritual.
We did not reshape the skull
to please the fickle eye.

WOMEN:    No need to sculpt the features
of a slave, Sirangan.
There is only one face for us.

MIDWIFE:    And now the three pairs
of gold earrings
and the band of bells
around the ankle.
She will make good music
when she walks,
our beautiful Princess.

DARAGANG MAGAYON:    There is only one face
demanded by the moulding eye.
We are all slaves of this master
who loves its handiwork
as I was loved
for my finely formed skull,
my skin they rubbed with scents
from the boats of the traders
with slanted eyes,

for my body nurtured vain
by the hands of slaves,
for my bound ankle chiming slim
and supple as my limbs
that held their eyes
when I danced in our feast
for the highest god Gugurang.

I wore too much gold as a child.
Around my head, a heavy band,
and on my ears, such glitter
presuming to be stars

upon some mortal heaven,
and about my neck and arms,
what shimmering each time I moved.

How they loved me,
how I loved me
for the sparkle on my skin.
I sometimes thought
we could not tell
the sheen of flesh from gold.
We were too certain of my body,
only of my body —
yes, there were doubts.
The Elders had more than eyes.

A coastal tribe, we were ravaged
by marauders from the sea.
They looted and burned our homes,
and dragged the women to their
        boats.
Our warriors fought the beasts,
but they always escaped,
leaving a trail of too much blood.
So the Elders spoke.

THE ELDERS:              We need princes to lead us.
                         How could our Datu Makusog
                         not have warrior-sons
                         instead of this preening thing?
                         See her arms, smooth and shapely.
                         How can they strain to bend
                         the bow? And those fingers
                         nimble for the loom
                         can hardly clutch a spear.

                         Datu Makusog, you need sons now.
                         Every day, another grey strand
                         on your crown, another quaver
                         clutching at your battle-cry.

The earth begins to call, our Datu.
Time to take another wife
who can spawn hunters.
Time to seed a new queen
before it is too late.
Enough grieving for Dawani.

DATU MAKUSOG:

There are women and women
for seeding. I have concubines,
all very young,
green enough for sons.
But Dawani was my only queen.
I will give you many sons
with my women.
I will give you hunters.

But my daughter will rule
when she grows up.
We hear of Urduja, of Sima,
women leading tribes,
and even Dawani ruled with me.
My daughter will learn.
In time. In due time.

THE ELDERS:

The beautiful one?
What does she know,
pampered so? Such softness.
We need a body with your name,
Datu Makusog. We need to believe
in its meaning: 'The Strong One'.
Will you fail this name,
our tribe, our great dead?
How could they sleep
without their seed
promising kins of strength?

DARAGANG MAGAYON: My father remembered well
my mother who ruled with him.

But ancient voices
plagued his ears
in wisdom's name.

THE ELDERS:       Exceptions, our Datu.
Those women-chiefs
are too few. Must you cast
your spear with them,
when there are sons
craving to be born?

DARAGANG MAGAYON:   The verdict was given
when I was barely four.
I could not rule.
So Father promised
he would make her queen
who bears his first son.
So his concubines
willed their wombs to swell.
Worshipping the *linggam*,
that rigid man-thing carved
in stone, they rubbed
breasts, bellies and groins
against such coldness.
How they wailed for sons.

I slowly shrank away
from all this clutching for warrior-
     heirs.
Was it because I never knew her
who might have wished for sons,
but had me instead —
thus slept the endless sleep?
So I thought about Dawani once,
so I thought about all those mothers
and their lust for sons.
Those mothers and unborn heirs,
they, too, were named.

But there were no sons.
Four daughters, my four half-sisters,
were born. And they refused to live
in a house that wished for sons
    alone.
One still-born, and three living
only for a day, as if the spirits
denied them breath.
In the old room where my mother
did not wake to hear me live,
I listened to my sisters' cries
that stopped in their throats.

Too sharp the halt;
the aching quiet keened.
I could not understand
why I let go of their stop
in my own throat,
and wailed like the women
who wished for sons.
They held each other in their grief.

WOMEN:

There are tiny feet that run
only in the ear,
running fast and away.
Always away.
And with each step that dulls,
a surge of words
that have no tongue.
*Ay,* this feeling of fog,
heavy and darkening.

SIRANGAN:

Enough of grief.
Once it was Dawani
and this motherless child,
and year after year
for four years,
the four daughters
and these orphaned mothers.

The womb has two faces.
Grace and curse,
life and death.
So its every enfolding throb
must also promise the sea,
a wave pushing away
the leap of desire
to gather the world
on our lap.

For who shall gather us
when we drown?
When our generous thighs
become too crowded?
We have to do our gathering.
We have to hold us on our lap.

DARAGANG MAGAYON: And so they rocked themselves
to a calm on their laps.
They picked herbs
to kill my father's seed.
Unknown to him,
they healed their bodies
with their hands.
Enough of the deathcurse
on every birth.
So my father had no son.
So the Elders had no warrior.
So my father, one day,
took me to hunt —

the break in the throat,
the deathdrool from the lips,
that almost human quiver
final in the flesh of prey,
and the hunter's proud bellowing,
his animal grunt.
I could not find strength
in a match of strength.

But my father fumed
about my fear of blood.

So came the break
between daughter and father.
He chastised me for being
only beautiful.
'How could you have the bones
of our great dead?'
I was disowned.
And he went to the women every
    night
with the fury of a sonless chief.
He had to win his wars
or lose his name.

The Strong One was growing old
while the pirates spawned.
But, again and again,
the women killed his seed.
Thus his ire against them:
'Cast away these barren ones!'
They became our household slaves,
while he took younger flesh.
But still there were no sons.
The earth refused to yield
when it declared
it was more than earth.

Hence my fate was shaped
upon his sonless fate.

THE ELDERS:      Make alliance with warrior-chiefs.
Dumaraog or Hokoman or Gat
    Ibal —
and why not the fearless Datu
    Pagtuga
of Isarog? Offer your daughter
to any one of them.
She will give us hunters.

| | |
|---|---|
| DATU MAKUSOG: | But she is only a child<br>and they are old men. |
| THE ELDERS: | They are scarred men.<br>Hardy men. We have need of them.<br>Why, have you gone soft, Datu<br>    Makusog?<br>Have you lost your name?<br>It is only a daughter<br>who can not hunt —<br>to save the tribe? |
| DARAGANG MAGAYON: | It was after the ritual of the *Halya*<br>when I overheard the Elders,<br>that night after my first bleeding<br>when Sirangan and the women<br>told me about the moon-eater,<br>the glutton Bakonawa<br>who waited patiently<br>for wombs to round. |

So I vowed to learn to hunt
the earthly likes of him,
to snatch the cunning
from their gaze,
and fist it while I dance
and dance them blind.
I would not be fodder
for old men who live to hunt.

I was twelve years old
and I knew fear —
the wound on my skirt,
the warm flow down my thighs,
and Bakonawa smelling it.
Like the scarred hunters
the Elders spoke about,
he hovered around my womb.

So I unbound my ankle,
loosed my hair, my neck and arms.
I stripped off my gold.
Without its weight,
the women in the ritual
of the *Halya*
danced with earth and wind.

I vowed to free this body
in the likeness of their bodies.
In single rhythm,
did we not dance before?
Time to learn
the tricks of Bakonawa,
to wrench him down from the sky
and meet him on my ground.

| YOUNG DARAGANG MAGAYON: | Father, teach me to hunt. |
|---|---|
| DATU MAKUSOG: | This is a surprise.<br>My child, you have decided well.<br>*Ay,* my beautiful warrior<br>who is well loved.<br>The Elders will approve. |
| YOUNG DARAGANG MAGAYON: | Approval for survival<br>is the hardest thing. |
| DATU MAKUSOG: | Now you understand.<br>Daughter, we hunt to eat.<br>We kill to live.<br>You are certainly of our clan,<br>my very own. |
| YOUNG DARAGANG MAGAYON: | Not yours, Father,<br>but mine.<br>And I have to protect |

|                                |                                              |
| ------------------------------ | -------------------------------------------- |
|                                | what is mine.                                |
|                                | Teach me to hunt.                            |
|                                |                                              |
| DATU MAKUSOG:                  | You keep mouthing riddles                    |
|                                | like a sullen old woman.                     |
|                                |                                              |
| YOUNG DARAGANG<br>MAGAYON:     | This tribe is now unsafe;                    |
|                                | my own father conspires against me,          |
|                                | because I am not a son.                       |
|                                | Now, I am only as good                        |
|                                | as my womb —                                  |
|                                | as my mother was, Father?                     |
|                                |                                              |
| DARAGANG MAGAYON:              | And he went white,                           |
|                                | his hair all-silver suddenly,                |
|                                | the years deepening on his face,            |
|                                | an old man gaping at his past                |
|                                | and present scourge —                        |

you whom I loved most,
why did you live the legacy
of a word, only the ancients' word,
when sentences rushed so
in your want for speech?
It is but a word, Father.
Your name is but
the briefest word.

How did it seal your lips
to seal my fate?
Do you not remember
how you held me then
when Mother slept
her endless sleep?

| SIRANGAN:      | It is a daughter, my Datu.        |
|                | Here is Daragang Magayon.         |
|                |                                   |
| DATU MAKUSOG:  | How tiny, Dawani.                 |

*Ay,* you lost your chance
to see this fragile thing.
I can easily hold her
with half my arm, my love.
From palm barely
reaching the elbow.

How spare the lives we make.
Our niggardly pulse,
our briefest urgencies.
A chance smear on the cheek,
so easily brushed away,
a sudden spurt of blood,
so readily stemmed,
a bird fallen from flight,
so simply shriveled,
as if it never was.

That you should die, Dawani,
is my curse.
What becomes of me?
What becomes of this?
How to sing this crying thing
to sleep. How to grow a lap
without a womb.

DARAGANG MAGAYON: I saw the past live in his eyes
as he whispered, 'No, it was not
        grief
because it was no son. Know this,
my child. It was not grief,
because you were no son.'
And he turned away quickly
and went out to hunt.
How we hide the real eye,
red-rimmed and fogged,
as it cowers from the hand of night.

As if it had not a darkness of its own.
My father's eye shrank
from whispers tinged with blood.
Old voices that droned on
about how my breasts were ripening
to suckle many sons,
or how my hips would broaden yet
to ease the birth of heroes.
Voices that snagged his heart
to make it beat their tongue.

So, at thirteen, I resolved
to grow intimate
with Okot, the god of the hunt.
I had to hide my womb
and grow a breast with scars.
I had to weave a hunter's tale
that could ensnare
the Elders dumb.
I stalked the forests
as I stalked their will.
I told them stories of my hunt.

My jungle trysts
with the kingdom of trees,
where sky had no reason to wince
at the rough outline of hills.
The green hair of hardwood women
softened the peaks,
as their feet firmed the loam.
I loved the way dawn
threaded through their hair.
*Ay,* filaments of soft burning.

Swift as an *amid,*
a wildcat in its leap,
I combed them with conviction.
My flesh became the colour of
        trunks,

deep-brown and scarred.
The tips of my hair even
hinted a black-green.
The Elders must have approved,
because the talk about my womb
was hushed for a time.
I told them many stories
woven in earthcolours.

They listened
and even asked me to sit
around their fire.
Then they called me
with another name,
Sadit ni Makusog,
Young of The Strong One.
And Father beamed with pride;
he had a woman-son.
But the Elders always asked for
    proof,
what game I chased,
how big, how good the wound.

Because I seldom killed my prey,
but stalked it well.
Remember, it was cunning
I had to learn,
more than killing.
'Look here, O Ancient Ones,
my game are stories
more than butchered flesh.'
I was thirteen and I had faith
in the warmth of their eyes.
But it must have been another gleam
or just the fire.

Later, I understood,
when in my preying for tales,
I met the earth-bound Bakonawa.

Not like his giant kin in the sky,
but a small man. Really.
And his chest did not ripple with
    scales.
Only scarred and hardened flesh
stretched across bones
to cage the heart.
How could it ripple then,
how could it beat?
There was a familiar gleam
in his watchful eyes.

DATU PAGTUGA:    Okot, god of the hunt!
Show me where that *amid* hides,
what tree. Hah! The bastard is faster
than the wind. Okot, I ask you,
let this be mine.

YOUNG DARAGANG    Old fool!
MAGAYON:    Nearly wounding me
with his arrow.
Is he blind,
or are all that move
animals in his eyes?

DARAGANG MAGAYON:    He stalked me then,
eyes darting about.
Their glint recalled other eyes
around a fire. I knew
I was the game,
so I combed the trees,
and quietly became a trunk,
a limb, a leaf —

DATU PAGTUGA:    A beautiful *amid*
on soundless feet!
And very young.
Whipping hair and thrusting

little angry breasts.
It is a good hunt after all.

YOUNG DARAGANG    You knew it was no animal
MAGAYON:          you stalked — !

DATU PAGTUGA:     What strong thighs.
                  Colour of trees.
                  *Ay,* silk of leaves.

YOUNG DARAGANG    You shall have war
MAGAYON:          on your hands.

DATU PAGTUGA:     War feeds from these hands,
                  my lovely game —
                  the hunt is war,
                  and Okot is a good ally.

YOUNG DARAGANG    Stop your rutting, old boar!
MAGAYON:          I am a princess,
                  and I will have your blood.

DATU PAGTUGA:     And I am Datu Pagtuga,
                  so you can have my seed —
                  what joy for you, what honour!

YOUNG DARAGANG    You have dug your grave, old man!
MAGAYON:

DARAGANG MAGAYON: The beast had smelled my womb.
                  We struggled — it was the *Halya*
                  without the music, a dance
                  for life. I stabbed the back
                  of his pressing thigh
                  with my dagger and fled.
                  I was *amid* resolving into eagle
                  as I raced his heaving form.
                  In his shrinking hardness,
                  he fumbled and lost his prey.

That was the hunt
they never believed.
I ran home and told them,
and their eyes lit up again,
brighter than the fires,
but they never believed.
Not to my face.
I told you I had stories
instead of game
for the Elders' ears alone,
because I could not bring home
enough carcasses
to feed unwhetted eyes.
I could only make them gleam.

This one story I brought home
with the wounding dagger
and the welts of lust
red on my skin,
but their eyes only burned it
a deeper red. Then a flood
of murmurings —
they asked for real game.
But I was the game.
They asked for blood.
I drew the blood.
I asked for justice.
How they stared.

They had not forgotten
my old name after all.
Daragang Magayon,
Beautiful Maiden
with a womb for sons,
with a breast for the lips
of heroes. That night,
Sirangan said they talked
long and late — they told
my father it was good
that I had met Pagtuga.

## III  PAGTUGA

DARAGANG MAGAYON: The hunt is war
where warriors stalk to win.
Where every outer muscle grows
  an ear
that heeds only its own chanting.
'Kill!' And death is too soon,
even before the blade
concludes the chant.
Somewhere in the marrow
of our hunting urge,
something dies.
There are no winners.

But how could we who even wring
an endless noon for rain
sharpen daggers for the kill?
Hear the gasp of green shoots
pushing through our bones
each time our blade is raised.
Listen to this little death within.
But maybe we are deaf
to the painful straining
of our inner skin.

Our green will is buried
much too deep for the eye.
This 'go!' in each cell
to split into cell
after breathing cell

is hidden from our preying eyes.
*Ay,* I wish our bodies skinned,
turned inside out.
Maybe we can touch
what we kill and kill again.

Tomorrow, I will die
by my own hands.
I will fight Pagtuga,
hunter against hunter —
but named as warrior now,
I can not leave unscathed.
I will also die by my own hands
as I have vowed to kill.
This inner skin will shrivel
at my battlecry.

Listen to more stories
that might justify
my warrior's rage.
Tales to make you think,
it is good, my change of name.
Daragang Magayon to Sadit ni
    Makusog.
From Beautiful Maiden
to the Young of The Strong One,
from woman to warrior,
womb and breast hidden now
in armour, my softness
hardening into a punishing lash.

But what of this new name?
This name that is still
my father's name.
Another baptism for vanities.
My old name, Daragang Magayon,
the ancients' legacy,
had none of muscle or mind,
because the Beautiful Maiden

must only please the eye.
And, now, a warrior's name
that carves a deathmark on my
    brow;
only cunning and strength for
    the kill.
No softness now.

So listen to another story
of baptism. Eight moons
after the struggle in the forest,
Pagtuga and my father met.
In separate hunts,
they shared a common chant.

DATU PAGTUGA:        Okot, god of the hunt,
                     can you hear the jungle-throb
                     of my old scars?
                     Every prey peels off the scabs
                     and wounds are raw again,
                     gaping open for another kill.
                     What is the gift this time?

DATU MAKUSOG:        A wild boar? A deer?
                     Okot, I hear you in the wind.
                     Have you chosen me again?
                     Listen to my bloodrush
                     promising to spill the blood of game
                     in your name, O Most Benevolent.
                     What is the gift this time?

DATU PAGTUGA:        A boar. Snared by the corner of
                         my eye.

DATU MAKUSOG:        A fat one. Unsuspecting swine.

DATU PAGTUGA:        Careful, feet.
                     Trust your stealth of paws.

| | |
|---|---|
| DATU MAKUSOG: | Ready, hands.<br>Clutch the spear with claws. |
| DATU PAGTUGA AND<br>DATU MAKUSOG: | And kill! |
| DARAGANG MAGAYON: | It squealed once,<br>rolled and grunted in surprise,<br>and was still — how they roared<br>as they sped for the prize.<br>As if it could run again. |
| DATU PAGTUGA: | Get your hands off my boar. |
| DATU MAKUSOG: | Your boar? It is my spear on<br>    the heart. |
| DATU PAGTUGA: | Surely, you see my arrow on<br>    the head. |
| DATU MAKUSOG: | Mine was the fatal wound.<br>I stopped the lifebeat. |
| DATU PAGTUGA: | My quiver was the faster one.<br>The first wound was mine. |
| DARAGANG MAGAYON: | Hunter against hunter,<br>they hunted for the answer<br>of their need:<br>Who was chosen by Okot?<br>Who is the better man?<br>Who is the killer?<br>We hanker for the guilt<br>when we hunger for the name.<br>But dead boars do not<br>baptise living men.<br>What power can be drawn<br>from carcasses? |

So they came to Rawis.
Our tribe was closest
to their battlefield.
Here, they set to share the boar,
and he saw me again.
Pagtuga awed by his *amid*,
the wildcat with the thighs
of trees — she who wasted
his gift of seed.
This prey named
by his hardness.

DATU PAGTUGA:     Who is she?

DATU MAKUSOG:     Daragang Magayon,
Princess of Rawis.
The Young of Makusog.
My very own warrior.

DATU PAGTUGA:     Princess?

YOUNG DARAGANG     We met eight moons ago
MAGAYON:     when you lost your prey.
Or have you forgotten?

DATU PAGTUGA:     Daragang Magayon.

YOUNG DARAGANG     That look on your face —
MAGAYON:     the hunter thinks the *amid*
can forget, Datu Pagtuga?
How can its blood congeal
when it nurses its wound
against healing?
It can not grow scabs
unlike the scar on your thigh.

DATU MAKUSOG:     I hear you have met before.

| | |
|---|---|
| DATU PAGTUGA: | How not to meet?<br>Your daughter hunts. It seems<br>we stalked the same prey.<br>A story like ours today, my friend.<br>But I did not know<br>she was a girl — such forest<br>cunning for a girl.<br>Truly The Young of Makusog.<br>What great honour<br>for my pleasured eye. |

Okot is wise to lead me
to the boar and to you, Datu
    Makusog,
to your tribe. He spurred my feet
and winged my eyes —
*ay,* your princess is most beautiful.
Okot is generous; now so am I.
You may have the whole boar.
It is a present from a happy man.

As for your princess,
it would be my pleasure
to hunt with her again.

| | |
|---|---|
| YOUNG DARAGANG<br>MAGAYON: | Hah! What delusion!<br>Were you the last boar<br>in the forest, I would not<br>stalk your precious meat. |
| DARAGANG MAGAYON: | What my father knew<br>was the story of the Elders,<br>    not mine.<br>Pagtuga was the favoured one,<br>he who stalked young virgins.<br>My name was a leap<br>of red in his loins.<br>Daraga. The Maiden.<br>Magayon. The Beautiful. |

Ours was a time when a bride
was ravished first in ritual
before the marriage night
to ease the seeding
by her groom.
But Pagtuga was different,
Sirangan cautioned me.
The ravishing was his alone.
*Ay,* the primacy of his blade.
His was always the first wound.

SIRANGAN:                    He chooses them very young,
his many wives.
There is a ritual for them.
They wash their hair
in kadlum leaves
before he takes them to his bed.
Their hair must not lose
the leaf-scent for three days,
a proof of maidenhood.

YOUNG DARAGANG            This fragrance of virgins
MAGAYON:                     stirs his ancient limpness young?
More promise for his seed;
his forty fruits are not enough.

SIRANGAN:                    The greed for fruit is as vicious
as the greed for the bed.
Be warned, Daragang Magayon.
Remember Bakonawa.
He watches his prey;
he comes every season.

YOUNG DARAGANG            I should learn his cunning?
MAGAYON:

SIRANGAN:                    You should know his eyes
with your own eyes.

Be warned, Daragang Magayon,
and do not sleep.

DARAGANG MAGAYON: My ageing nurse sang again,
not lullabies, but chants for waking,
while he vowed
I would be wived to him.
I did not see them,
but I did hear their ripple,
the scales about his loins,
as he came to our tribe
to thrust his spear
at my father's stairs.

Asking for my hand,
he brought gold, pearls and heads
from the hunt as gifts.
The Elders talked about my womb
      again
and sons, the likes of Pagtuga.
Meanwhile, the pirates
hunted our tribe every season,
but father was too old
to battle them. Too much blood
pounded on our doors.

WARRIORS: We are tired of the lull
of too much wakefulness.
Each night, we wait
for pirates. And our kins
wait with us on their beds;
always, there is no sleep.
In their fast boats,
those hunters sail our minds,
and pull to shore, our eyes.

FIRST WARRIOR: My youngest cries.
The back of his hand
wipes tears away,

but not the shadows
lurking on his lids.

SECOND WARRIOR:    My mother hides
her battle every time
I shut the door behind me.
But I see blood in her gaze.
She watches for pirates
with me, eyes frayed
from too much wiping off
the endless night.

THIRD WARRIOR:    My aged father passes his hands
on his white hair
again and again,
raking away the long wait.

FIRST WOMAN:    My second son watches for pirates;
my firstborn they killed yesterday.
Our neighbor has given up
   many sons,
all of them — but the pirates
   still come.

SECOND WOMAN:    I smell blood each time
my husband leaves.
But I do not know whose
it shall be. Perhaps,
it is mine.

THIRD WOMAN:    How my daughter cringes.
She knows the smell,
she who saw her sisters
dragged to the boats.
She knows they are not coming
   back.

SECOND WOMAN:    My baby stifles a whimper

at the sound of boats.
He stares about with eyes
red from the burning of houses.
He has such old eyes.

THE ELDERS:      So what can you do, Datu
                     Makusog?
                 You with your great name —
                 we need allies. Why not Datu
                     Pagtuga?
                 His spear is at your daughter's steps.
                 Betroth her then — surely, he will
                 offer more than gold and pearls.
                 His army is every pirate's doom.

DATU MAKUSOG:    Give me time.
                 I must speak to my daughter.

THE ELDERS:      Time? There is no time.
                 You are father to only one girl.
                 Do you know how it is to sire
                 many lost sons?

OLD MEN:         Do you know how a gash is cut
                 before it even heals? Son after son,
                 we have lost. But you have
                 only one daughter
                 protected by many sons, our sons,
                 your slaves of the blood.
                 Our Datu, do you know
                 how it is to bruise
                 a bleeding groove?

WOMEN:           Whoever said it could heal?
                 This sharp rent shuts like eyes.
                 The lids drop in sleep,
                 but nudge them once,
                 and they wake staring,

bare to the sky,
glazed by the heat.
Always wet;
always raw.

These are our eyes
scarred by death.
They memorised the final heave
of breast, the desperate pursuit
    of air
that does not even run away,
and the dreaded flicker of the torch
in the pupil of our dying.
Then the night,
the cold stare of night.

THE ELDERS:        The tribe is your first family,
      our Datu.
They have gathered food for
      your table
where they never sat,
but must you feed on them?
Enough this feast of blood;
they are not fodder for your throne.
Be warned. The master could be
      served
as final course. Heed
the angry men and women
at your door.

DATU MAKUSOG:      This legacy of a name,
this walking a tightrope of a word.
I will speak to my daughter.

DARAGANG MAGAYON:  He asked me,
a broken man begging his child.
He pleaded then fumed then cried.
My old father torn

between tribe and kin.
In my mind, I chopped my
        breasts off
and carved out my womb,
spilling this curse on women,
gutting my name. How I
wished a dagger would rise
between my thighs.

But is it not that men
were cursed as well
and named to die in war?
Well honoured though in death,
unlike us who wait.
Each day, our women died
from the emptiness of doors.
Or, waiting, they were vanquished;
lips, breasts, groins wived
to the teeth of the beast.

Why should I rage then against
        my body?
There is enough raging against it.
Rage of hands and eyes
that mould the flesh into names
they juggle in display.
Who is the author of names?
It is he who doles out words
that sear the lifetime of the slave.
The master with the branding hand.

The likes of Pagtuga,
a name that means eruption,
ire of volcanoes.
Loin-furnace shaping
only weapons of war.
It melts bones and
fashions them into blades
that cleave the youngness

from the hands of warrior-sons,
boys enslaved by the father.

I argued against the masters
for my life. But it was only one life.

YOUNG DARAGANG
MAGAYON:

I can be warrior at fourteen
like all the other boys.
Did you not call me
The Young of The Strong One?
Did you not know
my cunning in the hunt?
Give me a fair battle now.
If I should die,
let it not be by my other name,
Daragang Magayon,
that only waits to be uttered
by the pulse of his loin.

THE ELDERS:

We remember your cunning
in telling many stories.
Daragang Magayon,
why muddle this urgency
with the simple question of a name?
You are the ruler — protect your
    brood.
A Datu does what the tribe asks
    of him;
a princess does what her sire asks
    of her.

DARAGANG MAGAYON:

I was only one daughter,
the princess of a tribe
that lost sons, fathers and daughters.
Who am I to be untouched
    by blood?
It was not just.
But I chose to bleed

by the blade,
and they would not let me.
My name was their choice.
Wife, not warrior;
the bed, not the blade.

But all of us suffer
both bed and blade.
All of us daughters waiting
to be dragged by strange hands.
All of us unarmed
and crouching from the dark.
All of us who are baptised
by our wombs. And cut in its name.
All of us who are not sons.

How wide our battlefield,
but how narrow our palms,
always unfurled, always vulnerable.
The master decides
there are no fists for us.
No wonder, even in our dance,
we turn only with open hands.
No clutching of the wind for us;
leave all the clutching to the sons.

So the *Sandugo* was celebrated.
My father and Pagtuga drew
    and drank
each other's blood in ritual.
The bloodbrothers sealed my fate.
Once again I was named
with their choice of name,
Agomon ni Pagtuga,
The Betrothed of Pagtuga.
The verdict was final.
In two years, I was to be his wife.

Then the final battle against pirates.
Our drums and battlecries rising,
as if the heavens demanded
that we peak at its door.

FIRST WARRIOR: The itch-pain of my fingers,
slave to the blade.

SECOND WARRIOR: The snarl brimming from my throat
that can not swallow rage.

THIRD WARRIOR: The lunge! This strange body
leaping from my body for the kill.

FOURTH WARRIOR: The thrust into flesh.
This ripping of his heart
before he quells my pulse.

WARRIORS: Gut the earth, the sea,
let the nightsky bleed!
Gut the earth, the sea,
let the fury seed!

DARAGANG MAGAYON: And the shores became a tomb
for all.
*Ay*, help me flesh these bones,
remnants of that night.
I wish them dreams
of earth and sea
without the marrow-ache
of questions worn thin
from asking and asking.
Who put the blade on their hands?
The master did.
But who clenched the blade?

WARRIORS: Datu Makusog!
Datu Pagtuga!

|  | Our great warriors. |
|  | Rawis, our tribe, our people! |
|  | No pirates will walk your shores |
|  | again. |

DATU MAKUSOG:  Datu Pagtuga, brother,
I owe you my tribe.

DATU PAGTUGA:  You have my blood
and I have yours. You think
I would allow it spilled?

DATU MAKUSOG:  We can all sleep again.

WARRIORS:  Yes, we can rest.
Too much red
wearies the eyes.

DATU PAGTUGA:  Triumph begets triumph.
Do you not think so, brother?

DATU MAKUSOG:  Yes, the pirates can not come back.
Not from this bleeding earth,
not from the sea that swallowed
them.

DATU PAGTUGA:  Two years.
It seems too long.

DATU MAKUSOG:  Not even in two years.
Not in a long time.
How can they come back?

DATU PAGTUGA:  But I will come back
for my bride, Datu Makusog.

WARRIORS:  Blow the *hamodyong*,
the buffalo horn!

It is time for the feast.

And the *tigsik!*

Here's to Datu Makusog,
The Strong One.
To Datu Pagtuga,
our bloodbrother.

We toast to these brothers.
They never run from the heat;
they lust like a bull.

DATU PAGTUGA:    I toast to Rawis.
How can the bee fly
from this sweetness?

Datu Makusog, we will remember.
After two years.

DARAGANG MAGAYON:    And who forgets?
Who can shut the lips
mumbling names of their dead?
Two years have passed
after a hard battle won,
yet the muttering
can only beget new names
for sacrifice.

Tomorrow, we fight Pagtuga,
my father's bloodbrother.
Another battle,
another bruising of the wound.
Perhaps the flesh is born with it;
perhaps, it knew the blade
before it even knew the womb.
And underneath the calm of skin
is another skin, always braced,
always waiting.

## IV  SIRANGAN

DARAGANG MAGAYON:  There is always another war
after every war.
And when the blades are buried,
there are more heroes.
Tending scars, their movements
are slow, begging tenderness
even from the wind. Gently, please,
air on broken skin — it stings.
Every day, it spins scabs,
but they are too thin.
And the loom is tired.

When the blades are buried,
there are more heroes.
And theirs is not courage
of a sudden flash
surging when the foe is close,
not the tightening of flesh
for that lethal blow.
It is a courage long
and drawn-out like a breath,
air endlessly pursuing air.

WOMEN:  They say we have won.
But I am looking for my son.
They say we have won.
But my boy has not come home.
They say we have won.

But I dig a tomb for him.
They say we have won.
How can a graveyard hear?

DARAGANG MAGAYON: Ears can grow from the gutted earth.
Press your own on it
and listen — it listens back,
aching for answers.

WOMEN: The answers to our daughters'
       wailing
in the boats that left?
The answers to our asking,
should we dig them graves?
There are no bodies to bury.
And there are no answers.
Between me and the earth,
the air is mute.

Outriggered, but its rush
can not go to sea;
lush with words,
but its tongue keeps unripening.
Between me and the earth,
the weave of grief is dumb.
Too narrow, too tight.
There is no breathing
in its warp and weft.

DARAGANG MAGAYON: The salt of the wind
became the taste of their words
that asked the sea
about the unburied ones.
After the funeral rite
for our slain warriors,
the mothers paced the shore
for days and nights,
waiting for the daughters
who disappeared.

How they waited.
The wind was their lips
ululating a dirge
they could never finish.
The sea was their breast
that leapt, nipples hardening
at the memory of girl-babies
whose own breasts now
are maybe bared somewhere,
suckling mouths too old for milk.

WOMEN:    The sliver of moon
could be the curve of her cheek,
and the beached seaweed,
her hair trailing with tales
she wishes to tell me.
The grains of brine
could be her trapped wailing,
and the persistent rush of wave
after wave, her voice
that wants to come home.

We have buried our sons,
brothers and husbands,
but how can we bury our daughters
who left in the looters' boats?
Can we gather the moon,
the seaweed, the brine
and the hum of the sea,
then bury them?
Tell us, Princess.
You whom we can see
and touch, tell us.

DARAGANG MAGAYON:    I could not answer.
After a war, there is guilt
in being alive.
I wished to quell it

with my impending fate.
I longed to tell them
I, too, would have my time.
I touched my rounding breasts,
remembering they were no longer
    mine.
But who was I to stamp my grief
upon these mothers' keening?

A princess. Alive. Beloved.
Her royal marriage bed waiting.
But how could I tell them
I would be dragged to it as well.
Another daughter, another spoil
    of war,
yet no mother to wait for me.
Only my dear Sirangan who knew
the price my father paid.
Her old voice chanted
bloodsongs for healing.

SIRANGAN:    The moonlit sea is sleep-talking
stories of the disappeared.
The crescent listens from above
as it begins to round into a
    new womb,
remembering the curve of the old.
It does not forget.
We are of moon-memory.

WOMEN:    How to bury the moon.

SIRANGAN:    When our fingers track the glint
across the water,
we sense the sheen of skin
of young women who danced
    with us
to drive the beast away.

When we lick the salt on our lips,
we taste the sweat of spent bodies,
if not the sharpness of decay,
beached upon some alien shore.

WOMEN:       How to bury the sea.

SIRANGAN:     We can not forget the disappeared.
We dare not forget the loss
lest we lose again.
Like the waxing orb, we recall
the old shape of the womb
and our will to guard it.
We are of moon-memory.

So let us gather the sliver
of silver, the seaweed, the brine
and the voice of the sea,
but not to bury them. Never.
Let us rub the silver on our eyes,
wash our hair in seaweed
and soak our skin in brine,
then grow a sea-voice.

WOMEN:       It may be calm where it is deep,
but waves always wail.

SIRANGAN:     We will not forget,
but we must begin to heal.
Let the glint repair the eyes.
Let the salt seep through
to sting the wounded inner skin
and weave scabs.
Let the voice swell into a sea-rage
for the time when it must stop
another plunderer.

*Ay,* let us heal. Remember,
we are of moonskin as well.

The shavings from the flesh
    that waned
are always recovered,
drawn back toward a centre
that is never lost.
Then we wax whole again.
Recall the tatters of skin,
ransom them from the dark,
and let us wax again.

DARAGANG MAGAYON: Sirangan encouraged touch,
this remembering of body
with salt and light and skin
on skin. She urged us
to rub the ailing flesh
with healer's hands straining,
as if to let palmskin
stretch over every gash.

SIRANGAN: Skin and eyes to be stung
    but salved
with a palmful of sea and moon.
Then the calm of pores.
These lips of the skin will shut,
and their unintelligible moans
will surge to the throat instead,
where they will gather
to become words.
Then the ache will not speak
against those who ache.
It will speak against itself.

DARAGANG MAGAYON: That time, I offered my palms
for their healing.
I offered to gather
the moon and the sea,
and rub them on their wounds.
But Sirangan took my hands in
    her own,

folded them, letting my palm
touch my other palm.

SIRANGAN:

*Ay,* the loneliness of thrones
saved by blood.
It cannot sit alone in light.
A shadow is cast
by too many bodies.

YOUNG DARAGANG
MAGAYON:

Sirangan, these hands will hunt
their bodies for aches to kill.

SIRANGAN:

I asked us to touch
our bodies with our hands.
Not the sea and the moon alone,
but a palmful of self
to rub over the self.

I touch your palm
unto your other palm.
Not by the other
can we heal, my child.
Forget illusions.

When they go to the sea,
I shall be with them,
but not above them.
I have my own healing.
I have my own past.

YOUNG DARAGANG
MAGAYON:

But you lost no one
in that battle. I am still here.

SIRANGAN:

You heard my story once,
or have you forgotten
that I have seen many battles?
That before your grandfather
took me to his house
to nurse your mother,

I was looking for my baby
that was taken by warriors
who pillaged our tribe.

Do you remember my old tale?
My son, a gift for their chief.
I never found him.
But I saw him each night,
him with the downward turn
of fishmouth unspeaking.
What young grief —
my lips took its shape
and lost speech as well.

YOUNG DARAGANG
MAGAYON:

But my mother's mouth on
        your breast
gave you back your words.

SIRANGAN:

Suckling eased the breast,
thus spilled out words,
but only because
I touched myself first
and remembered Sirangan.

YOUNG DARAGANG
MAGAYON:

It was her touch
that found your voice.
Let me offer my palms
to our women.
I will heal them.

SIRANGAN:

When they go to the sea,
I shall be with them,
but not above them.
You can be with us,
but not above us.
You ask too much.
Slaves of the blood,
we wounded our bodies

|  |  |
|---|---|
|  | for you — Princess, ask us not<br>to give you their healing. |
| YOUNG DARAGANG MAGAYON: | You censure me, Sirangan. |
| SIRANGAN: | For the heroics of the guilt<br>in being alive.<br>Daragang Magayon,<br>come with us<br>and watch us heal.<br>You shall have your time.<br><br>So remember with us.<br>Remember your body as your own.<br>Remember with touch.<br>Remember with voice that grows<br>with touch. Remember with us. |
| WOMEN: | In these waters, we listen<br>to our memories.<br>Shall the Princess listen as well? |
| SIRANGAN: | She must remember with us,<br>so she does not lose her voice. |
| FIRST WOMAN: | I was a daughter of a warrior. |
| SECOND WOMAN: | I was a wife of a warrior. |
| FIRST WOMAN: | I was a mother of three sons slain<br>in that battle. |
| THIRD WOMAN: | I was a mother of two daughters<br>in the boat that sailed away. |
| SIRANGAN: | I was a mother of a baby lost<br>long ago. |

143

| | |
|---|---|
| FIRST WOMAN: | But, now, I am Hara-hara. |
| SECOND WOMAN: | And you could be Takay. |
| THIRD WOMAN: | I am Bito'on. |
| FIRST WOMAN: | But you could be Damagan. |
| SIRANGAN: | Even Sirangan. |
| FIRST WOMAN: | *Ay,* once, I might have been a fish. |
| SECOND WOMAN: | Or a coral. |
| THIRD WOMAN: | Or an anemone. |
| FIRST WOMAN: | Or a stone. |
| SIRANGAN: | And we can be fish, coral, anemone, stone, even water. |
| FIRST WOMAN: | And we can rush to shore. |
| SECOND WOMAN: | And be the brine. |
| THIRD WOMAN: | And leap to air. |
| FIRST WOMAN: | And be the wind. |
| SIRANGAN AND ALL WOMEN: | How we speak many names beyond old names. We touch skin and shed skin. We remember self and find another. |
| DARAGANG MAGAYON: | In that ritual by the sea, they invoked the names |

of the creatures of Magindara,
goddess of the waterworld.
But invoked them as their own,
remembering their sea-lives,
curling their tongues around fish,
coral, anemone, stone, water, brine.
There, I also remembered
       many names,
but they were not mine.

Beautiful Maiden from my ancestors.
The Young of Makusog from
       my father.
The Betrothed of Pagtuga
from the hunter who vowed
to be my groom — all tightly
sheathing me like skin
alien to these bones.
But, as I listened to the chanting
of water-memories,
I ran my palms over each body
assigned to me — how each
strange skin fell away.
And a voice called out
a new name.

Woman. Hunter. Warrior.
Names only of a moment
as other words rang
more possibilities. Lover.
Mother. Earth. Bird. Fish.
*Ay,* I knew then I could lose
       my limbs
that gather a lover or murder
       a beast,
then grow wings to sweep the sky,
or fins to dive the deep.
Or my skin could swallow all limbs,
wings, fins — and I could close

unto myself whole as stone.

So Pagtuga need not be appeased.
It was just one of my names that was
promised him, a momentary self
I could dissolve. But how to know
this, when his is only one
unchanging, lonely name?
Pagtuga, meaning 'eruption',
a single spew of seeds.
And every germ
that touches fertile loam
must repeat his hunter's form.

So how could he have understood
the day I caused my father
to break his word?
Moons after we began
the sea-ritual, I shed
the name that made me his.
It was close to my sixteenth year
and Pagtuga was rubbing
his impatience, right after harvest.
He was a guest of my father.
And he was reeling with wine.

DATU PAGTUGA:            Only four moons to go
                        before you lie on my bed,
                        yet you never sit at my table
                        or even smile at me. My own *amid*,
                        wildcat of my hunt, how sleek
                        you have grown. And how proudly
                        you thrust those breasts and hips
                                at me.
                        Come, let me toast to you.
                        You have kept me too thirsty.

YOUNG DARAGANG           You shall not drink
MAGAYON:                 from your chosen cup.

DATU PAGTUGA: She has not changed
since that day of the hunt.
And her fury makes me swell
even more. Daragang Magayon,
why not feel for yourself
how well your fury dooms a man.

YOUNG DARAGANG You will not touch me.
MAGAYON:

DATU PAGTUGA: But you will —

YOUNG DARAGANG Remember who drew
MAGAYON: the blood in that hunt.

DATU PAGTUGA: The blood you drew
has flushed the loins.
How can I forget?

YOUNG DARAGANG The two years is not yet over.
MAGAYON: More blood might yet be drawn.

DATU PAGTUGA: It will not be mine, my betrothed.

DARAGANG MAGAYON: He grabbed my hand
forcing me to rub his ache.
The hunter preyed on me again —
and in my house!
Let the hunter die then in my house.
Having found my voice
with the women in the sea,
I remembered my rage.

We struggled. He was too drunk,
so his prey became the hunter.
That day could have set me free,
but just before my dagger found
    its mark,

his henchman came. Linog,
    the burly one.
Another name of death — Linog,
    meaning
'earthquake'. He struck me down.
But it was not I who died.

SIRANGAN:    You do not touch my child.

DATU PAGTUGA:    This dark-skinned slave
is ordering the chief?

YOUNG DARAGANG
MAGAYON:    I smell death, Sirangan.

SIRANGAN:    You will not take my child again.

DATU PAGTUGA:    What insolence! Linog,
this hag insults your master.

DARAGANG MAGAYON:    It was a very quick blow.
Linog did not hesitate at all.
The mind swallowed by the beast
becomes more monstrous than
    the beast.
She could have been his mother;
she could have rocked him
in her younger arms,
but she had defied the master.
Linog only saw the drunken chief
who tried to explain the blood
to the gathering crowd.

DATU PAGTUGA:    She attacked me.
The old slave lost her mind.
See the dagger in her hand?

YOUNG DARAGANG
MAGAYON:    Father, look hard at the truth.

148

| DATU PAGTUGA: | Brother, the dagger is proof. |
|---|---|

| DATU MAKUSOG: | It is no brother who murders in<br>my house. |
|---|---|

| DATU PAGTUGA: | Brother, she attacked me. |
|---|---|

| DATU MAKUSOG: | It is no brother<br>whom I shall take prisoner.<br>Warriors — ! |
|---|---|

| DATU PAGTUGA: | What jest! You expect a chief<br>to pay for the death of a slave?<br>You will punish the brother<br>who saved your throne?<br>What short memory, Datu Makusog.<br>You are asking for war. |
|---|---|

| DATU MAKUSOG: | Only because you struck the<br>first blow. |
|---|---|

| THE ELDERS: | *Ay,* mercy. No more war, our Datu. |
|---|---|

| DATU PAGTUGA: | Listen to your Elders, brother. |
|---|---|

| THE ELDERS: | We do not wish to fight.<br>But we shall not let this murder<br>go unpunished. Datu Pagtuga,<br>you owe us a life. Pay us back<br>with another slave. |
|---|---|

| YOUNG DARAGANG<br>MAGAYON: | But what of the true story?<br>Why must an old woman<br>wield a blade at them? |
|---|---|

| DARAGANG MAGAYON: | 'She must have lost her mind,'<br>thus replied the Elders, asking,<br>'Why should an old slave drag us |
|---|---|

to war? Why should a mere
woman endanger the tribe?
And why ask the master
to yield for her death?'

Father listened to them again,
even if his breast
swelled with answers.
He set the murderers free,
but broke the blood oath.
He vowed there would be
    no marriage
after four moons.

Meanwhile, the women raged
over the death of Sirangan.
They chanted in tongues
of fish, anemone, coral,
water and stone — as if
the disappeared had come home
to be buried. An old woman,
the murdered slave,
was reason for a grave.

So we keened the *Katumba*,
the funeral song finally finished.
At last, here was a body to bury.
Thus we invoked the creatures
of Magindara — this time,
to lead Sirangan home.

WOMEN:          *Ayyyy*, Sirangan,
there is a cradle in the sea.
It rests on the back of a fish.

FIRST WOMAN:    My fins quiver
at babydreams
rocking.

150

| | |
|---|---|
| WOMEN: | There is a cradle in the sea.<br>It sails past anemone. |
| SECOND WOMAN: | My hundred fingers<br>curl around sleepgurgles<br>passing. |
| WOMEN: | There is a cradle in the sea.<br>It brushes against fire corals. |
| THIRD WOMAN: | My porous bones<br>draw in the bubblebreath<br>humming. |
| WOMEN: | *Ayyyy,* Sirangan,<br>we sail the cradle home<br>with you. We are water. |
| | We sink the cradle and you<br>deep beyond grief.<br>We are stone. |
| | But warm. Skin-smooth<br>and promising wings.<br>We are bird. |
| | Hear the flapping<br>from the navel of the sea. |
| | Where the life-cord<br>is cut, there stirs<br>a rumour of rising. |
| YOUNG DARAGANG<br>MAGAYON: | Rising. In my throat, too, rising.<br>Women of Rawis,<br>there are too many words<br>about the shame of my kind,<br>we of the lighter skin,<br>we of the bloodied throne.<br>We do not see how underneath |

our headgears coloured by rank,
and beyond gradations
of flesh-tint — all skulls,
all bones, once bleached,
are always pearly white.
And nameless in the sun.

But how to know this
when skin and bone do not connect.
Between fleshcap and skull,
a dark space sits.
Its feral teeth
whittle the head.
Whittle thoughts to shape.
Whittle names assigned.
Woman. Man.
Slave. Master.
Dark. Light.

We look upon
this body of Sirangan
who shall be paid
by another body —
for a future kill
at the whim of the master?
Just another nape exposed
to the itch-pain of fingers,
god of the blade.
You say there stirs a rumour
rising from the navel of the sea.
It also rises in my throat.

WOMEN:                          We are water.
                                We are stone.
                                We are bird.

                                We float.
                                We bury.
                                We fly.

| | |
|---|---|
| YOUNG DARAGANG MAGAYON: | I take off this coloured silk around my head. Bury it. I cut my hair. Bury it. I was too heavy for flight. |
| WOMEN: | She is no princess. She is no beautiful maiden. She is not the young of her father. She is not the betrothed of the murderer. |

WOMEN:

She is no princess.
She is no beautiful maiden.
She is not the young of her father.
She is not the betrothed
of the murderer.

She is water.
She is stone.
She is bird.

DARAGANG MAGAYON:

Our mourning for Sirangan
lasted for ten days.
I took off the coloured cloth
that marked my head,
and cut my hair in the ritual
of the *Sanggol.* More than an act
of grief it was. Without the weight
of cloth and hair, fleshcap eased
closer to the skull and clung to it.
Enough this whittling of bones.

And the women buried cloth and
    hair
with Sirangan. Then they gathered
    me,
mothers recovering lost daughters.
Thus my skin was stroked by
    many palms
that sang with me the selves
I touched and remembered.
I am water. I am stone. I am bird.
I float. I bury. I rise.

YOUNG DARAGANG
MAGAYON:

I take off this coloured silk
around my head. Bury it.
I cut my hair. Bury it.
I was too heavy for flight.

## V   ULAP


DARAGANG MAGAYON:   There is a jar of earthtones.
Red almost brown almost black.
Like several skins flushed
under each other, imagining
how to be all, yet none of each.
This is the house of her bones.
I know they are pearly grey to white
like the bones of my mother.

Sirangan in a jar. Dawani in a jar.
Their tombs are intimate.
They are my colour.
If I rest my ear against them,
I would hear them sing
my skin. I have two mothers
and they sing my skin.

WOMEN:   Sky gives you back your eyes,
splinterless as the moon.
Earth gives you back your lips
to fruit with words.
Sea gives you back your breasts
without the welts.
Gives you back.

Because you touched
how hollow the sockets,
how barren the mouth,
how breasts were marked

redly, redly, redly.
But you remembered
beyond red. You are in love
with the rainbow.

DARAGANG MAGAYON: Song of gifts.
When voices are generous,
they are all colours.
I have many mothers.
They are all colours.
They have many voices
in song of gifts.

WOMEN: Eyes splinterless as the moon,
lips to fruit with words,
breasts without the welts.

DARAGANG MAGAYON: Listening to the women
sing on the shore
was like listening to Dawani
and Sirangan in their jars.
We buried my nurse beside
    my mother
in earthenware on the beach.
Then the sea memorised me,
eyes, skin, voice and all.
It refused to forget
what I refused to forget.
We had a daily pilgrimage
to the tombs.

I remember now how I rose
before each first light
to run against my grief.
I could not outrun it.
It was the salt in my eyes,
lips and skin, the sand clinging
to my soles, the wind flogging
my skull as if it willed

each strand of hair to ache.
And as I paced the burial ground,
a cry always gashed the air.
At first, I thought it was the earth
waking, wild from its seabed.

But as I threw myself
over the tombs,
my hoarseness told me
it was only the tide in my throat.
Then the following calm.
I waited for the jars to sing,
'eyes splinterless as the moon,
lips to fruit with words,
breasts without the welts.'
Then I sang with them,
as if to heal the air
I have just ripped.

I used the gifts of my mothers
to remember my many bodies
and colours, clear again and burning.
Woman. Warrior. Fish. Coral.
Anemone. Brine. Earth. Bird.
I chanted these names around
the graves. I danced them:
Yellow-armed, red-finned,
green-boned, blue-fingered,
saltwhite-nippled, black-bellied,
brown-winged me whirling sand
and whirling off the grief
until I hit water.

In a tryst with Magindara,
goddess of the waterworld,
the sea became all colours
as I swam for miles,
spanning waves and centuries
of touching and untouching.

A momentary curling of my arms
around a crest, before it curled
   me in,
only to unfurl and foam away,
before it loved me back again.
It loved me clean,
yet never washed off
my shock of pigments.
It flaunted them instead.

My blue-black-green-red-
yellow-brown-white skin
of a remembered goddess.
But, one day, her sea turned
a deep grey. Season of storm
grey. Almost grief grey.
I was swimming against
its greyness, flashing
my colours, when I heard
the women's song again
in the voice of a man.

| | |
|---|---|
| YOUNG DARAGANG MAGAYON: | Who goes there? |
| ULAP: | Sky gives you back your eyes. |
| YOUNG DARAGANG MAGAYON: | Who dares sing our song? |
| ULAP: | Sea gives you back your breast. |
| YOUNG DARAGANG MAGAYON: | Show yourself. |
| ULAP: | Your saltwhite nipples. |
| YOUNG DARAGANG MAGAYON: | Curse your eyes! |

| ULAP: | They wear a splinter<br>of your many colours. |
|---|---|
| YOUNG DARAGANG<br>MAGAYON: | Who are you? |
| ULAP: | Ulap, a freeman from the Tagalog.<br>Please sheath that knife —<br>I mean no harm. I like your song. |
| YOUNG DARAGANG<br>MAGAYON: | Our song is ours, intruder. |
| ULAP: | Green bone song. |
| YOUNG DARAGANG<br>MAGAYON: | Spying on me? |
| ULAP: | Red fin song. |
| YOUNG DARAGANG<br>MAGAYON: | Who sent you? |
| ULAP: | The wind. I am running from<br>the wind. |
| YOUNG DARAGANG<br>MAGAYON: | Fool not with me, stranger. |
| ULAP: | You are the wind's kin,<br>you with the knife — ? |
| YOUNG DARAGANG<br>MAGAYON: | The wind's kin? |
| ULAP: | Two days I watched you.<br>I thought you were different. |

| | |
|---|---|
| YOUNG DARAGANG MAGAYON: | Your back is bleeding! |
| ULAP: | I should have known that the wind sings. |
| | He sings everywhere with the slaughtered fowl on his whitest hair. |
| | I remember the fire in his breath — |
| DATU PAGTUGA: | You must pay for that life you took. |
| ULAP: | It is for a meal. I am lost and have not eaten for days. |
| DATU PAGTUGA: | Feed on my fowl? |
| ULAP: | No one bans the forest from a famished man. |
| DATU PAGTUGA: | My forest is no friend to hungry strangers. |
| ULAP: | Unhand me, then I can explain. |
| DATU PAGTUGA: | Do you know how a fowl runs — |
| ULAP: | But I am no thief! |
| DATU PAGTUGA: | When it runs for its life? It runs-flies-runs, and prays to the wind to carry it away. |
| ULAP: | Take back this fowl then — |

| | |
|---|---|
| DATU PAGTUGA: | Will you pray to the wind — ? |
| ULAP: | My back! |
| DATU PAGTUGA: | I am the wind<br>that cuts through skin. |
| ULAP: | Bastard! |
| DATU PAGTUGA: | Now you are free — |
| ULAP: | I kill for life! |
| DATU PAGTUGA: | To run — |
| ULAP: | I must run! |
| DATU PAGTUGA: | With the wind after you. |
| ULAP: | Run! |
| DATU PAGTUGA: | You prayed to it — |
| ULAP: | Run! |
| DATU PAGTUGA: | To carry you away. |
| DARAGANG MAGAYON: | Ulap fled with a wounded back<br>and intimations of the death-throes<br>of the fowl he killed.<br>How he prayed against the wind.<br>Then he reached the river Yawa,<br>where a windless night crept,<br>a warm solace of shadows.<br>It was the river of our tribe,<br>which Pagtuga dared not cross<br>for fear of ambush.<br>He had just killed Sirangan. |

Then Ulap followed the river
to where it meets the sea.
There he heard me sing
with my mothers.
He listened and watched
for two days. He was a stranger
who eyed the knife
at my belt with suspicion.
But, in his fever, he must have
heard all my colours,
must have believed enough
to sing with them.

His stranger's voice
took me by surprise,
so I bared my knife.
Caution is ever rough-edged.
I have long aped the death-lunge
of the forest from the time
I was hunted, and the broken
    betrothal
had fired each vigilant pore;
thus the swing of my blade
against a helpless man —
but do we all turn into
monsters at the edge of fear?

I wondered about my kinship
with the wind, then dismissed
the thought. I hid my knife
and led him to the water.
I washed his back, my hand tentative
on wincing skin. He kept muttering
about the wind as the grey sky
suddenly lighted blue and pealed.
There is no known patience
    of storms.
They do not wait for strangers
to become less strange.

| | |
|---|---|
| ULAP: | The wind is here. |
| YOUNG DARAGANG MAGAYON: | I will take you home. |
| ULAP: | It is the colour of fire.<br>Blue fire. |
| YOUNG DARAGANG MAGAYON: | It is only the lightning. |
| ULAP: | Its voice is a drum.<br>Death drum. |
| YOUNG DARAGANG MAGAYON: | It is only the thunder. |
| ULAP: | It will carry us away.<br>Both of us. |
| YOUNG DARAGANG MAGAYON: | We are too heavy for the wind. |
| DARAGANG MAGAYON: | Then I kept him home<br>amidst my father's silence<br>and the Elders' protests.<br>'He is a spy sent by Pagtuga.<br>He has plotted against us<br>since the betrothal was broken.<br>There is war in the air.<br>We should stop this<br>dangerous alliance.'<br>Strangely enough,<br>my father did not protest.<br>Ulap was sheltered.<br><br>I wondered about my sire's<br>change of heart — a common |

stranger in the princess' hut?
Must have been his silent
defiance of the Elders and the stories
that he once believed.
Perhaps, an apology
to his estranged daughter
or a seal of the broken betrothal.

In that season of storms,
the stranger's wound and mine
were washed by the monsoon.
I was a few days away
from sixteen years,
growing up and growing out
of scabs. It seemed a stretching
of age as I visited the tombs
of my mothers by day
and listened to his fevered
breathing by night.

I told them about him
and his long sleep,
about how I sat my grief
and anger down on the beach
each time I swam,
their sullen grey displaced
by many names shifting in my body.
A motley of voices and colours,
each one with a chance
to sing her momentary space:

Woman. There are nights
when the sea ripples
in my thighs
and my fingers
become urgent fishes,
like that time
I changed his clothes
drenched in feversweat.

He muttered about the wind
and flailed an arm,
brushing my belly luminous.

Warrior. The steady furnace
of my loin also sharpens
the edge of thought
into a definitive swing of blades.
And my whetstone ears
tune the metal timbre
to the ring of my voice
that hurled 'No!' at Pagtuga.
Slingstone-no right between
his eyes devouring my burning.

Coral. Dancing fire frozen
into intricate bone
with a million eyes sucking in
the rush of saltwater.
Filigreed yet stone-rough,
I hold knowledge as deep
as my home. And, out of it,
my vessel lies calm on the sand.
Wind can only pass through
    my body,
even if it desired to snatch me
with rodent teeth.

Anemone. Many-fingered,
I live on drawing in
all stray swimmers.
Needing or answering to need,
my breath curls in
as tendrils beckoning for touch
or for them who seek touch.
Mother of the deep, soft
and sensual in its invitation,
I could keep my guests
from ever leaving.

Brine. Crystal of the eye.
Winking, teasing shard
that trapped the sun.
Or my memory that congealed
into a grain of silver-white.
Eye-rain, perhaps,
that has forgotten
how to run. I need
the sea to remember
how liquid grief can be.

Fish. My nipples
or the tips of my toes
in perpetual quiver of fins.
Or a diver beyond body-
shiver. Not fins alone,
but spirit, silver-blue
yet turning black
as I plunge deeper
to the end of all thoughts.

Earth. I am black and warm
in heat, and drenched darker
in rain. I am the lap of the world
and the master of soles.
I teach step and unstep.
I tell green stories
flushed into every colour
after the monsoon.
My womb is a rainbow
fragrant as dung
in a summer night.

Bird. I have more than
two wings, but two eyes
can only think in pairs.
My other wings flap
visibly in my breast.
Here, I rise as a swell

of blood, staining the sky
crimson — I always claim it
coloured with the break
or end of day, because I fly
in full-circles, rising-roosting.

I let the sky rest,
as once I let my grief
and anger rest,
while Ulap slept
in a different season.
I healed well as he healed well.
Kins of the hunt, preyed upon
by a shared enemy, we listened
to each other's breathing,
while the Elders passed
judgment on the princess
who had loved a commoner.

FIRST ELDER:        It is her passing fancy,
                    her initiation to the body.

SECOND ELDER:       Her eyes are moons
                    when she gazes at him.

THIRD ELDER:        She has opened her legs
                    to a man below her station.

FIRST ELDER:        Whored with the earth!

SECOND ELDER:       But Pagtuga demands to be first.

THIRD ELDER:        No one must know.
                    The slaves in this household
                    must be warned
                    against their tongue.

SECOND ELDER:       She will not pass Pagtuga's test.

|  | Her hair will lose the smell of *kadlum* leaves before she lies on their marriage bed. |
|---|---|

FIRST ELDER: But her father has vowed
there will be no marriage.

SECOND ELDER: Pagtuga saved us in a war.
The warrior deserves his prize.

FIRST ELDER: There could be another war
should we break our vow.

THIRD ELDER: We must caution our Datu.
We must plead for our lives.
What is one woman
against a whole tribe?

DARAGANG MAGAYON: Too many whisperings,
the chirping of old birds
fretting about their bone.
I thought, perhaps,
it is wise to make
their fears come true.
I will part my thighs,
but not for them.

'Never out of spite.
I only wish to listen closely
to the sea in my thighs,'
one of my voices teased
as I bent over the naked stranger
who had just woken
from a long sleep.

YOUNG DARAGANG
MAGAYON: You have healed well.

| | |
|---|---|
| ULAP: | I am forever indebted. |
| YOUNG DARAGANG MAGAYON: | Thank your story. |
| ULAP: | I do not understand. |
| YOUNG DARAGANG MAGAYON: | Too much to understand. |
| ULAP: | I want to know many things. May I start with your name? |
| YOUNG DARAGANG MAGAYON: | I have many names. |
| ULAP: | Red fin. It quivered above my face. |
| YOUNG DARAGANG MAGAYON: | Your fevered skin. |
| ULAP: | Green bones. They were luminous. |
| YOUNG DARAGANG MAGAYON: | Only a seaweed dream. |
| ULAP: | Brown wings. A thousand beating. |
| YOUNG DARAGANG MAGAYON: | Mere windtalk. |
| ULAP: | Saltwhite nipples. |
| YOUNG DARAGANG MAGAYON: | A most forward tongue does not sit well |

with an embarrassed flush.

ULAP: Saltwhite.

YOUNG DARAGANG
MAGAYON: White of the foam.

ULAP: I should like to see
how white.

YOUNG DARAGANG
MAGAYON: White of your eyes.

ULAP: I should like to know
how much of salt.

DARAGANG MAGAYON: I was the brine then
at the wicked brink
of being water again,
conjuring its seabed.
Young and old all at once
with a stranger yet,
but whose body had lost
its strangeness
as I nursed it back to health.

But what about Pagtuga
who spoke with the same
    boldness,
but stirred not desire?
His voice did not limn
with the pulse in my throat.
*Ay,* more than loinsong
fires the skin;
where thoughts
rub each other,
the sparks begin.

I made my choice
after three nights of talk.
I let the brine dissolve
upon a tongue that wondered
how much of the sea
hardened my nipples,
while mumbling my name-
lessness over and over.
In his throat, a cricket
eluded sleep.

YOUNG DARAGANG MAGAYON: There are palmwings
above the monsoon —

ULAP: Warmly puddleful,

YOUNG DARAGANG MAGAYON: And darkly rippled,

ULAP: Swimming-singing,
'finquiver, finquiver'

YOUNG DARAGANG MAGAYON: In air I dare,

ULAP: Yet dare not
breathe-
break.

YOUNG DARAGANG MAGAYON: Wish it broken.

ULAP: Shards are liquid.

YOUNG DARAGANG MAGAYON: Shards are salt.

ULAP: Shards are sweet.

| | |
|---|---|
| YOUNG DARAGANG MAGAYON: | Wipe them not. |
| ULAP: | They dry in heat. |
| YOUNG DARAGANG MAGAYON: | Brined again. |
| ULAP: | Whole again. |
| YOUNG DARAGANG MAGAYON: | Beached again. |
| DARAGANG MAGAYON: | Thus we moored to summer. I walked him to the tombs and presented him to my mothers. 'This is my lover, but he is not mine.' He told my mothers the same. The anemone curled a tendril around a fish, but not to feed. The coral let the water through, the earth pushed out the seed and the wings claimed other journeys. |

Ulap was a newly freed slave
on his way to the south
where he wished to live
away from his tribe. Like him,
I had just freed myself then
from my other name, Daraga —
Maiden. Between my legs,
I had gathered red flowers.
But I knew these hands
must learn beyond red.
There are other colours
and rituals beyond gathering.

## VI  WARANG PANGARAN

DARAGANG MAGAYON:  My words are moonless,
but they have mouths.
And the night has ears,
so it cannot sleep.
It listens to all my stories
that bared their teeth
to cut the belly
of the moon-eater open.
Light shall be retrieved
from the face of the sun.
The east will soon be red,

the colour of the wound
on my skirt when I was twelve,
or eyes remembering the dead,
the flowers between my legs,
and, soon, the edge of the blade.
*Ay,* this night is too long
and impoverished of colour.
But tomorrow, it will have wound,
eyes, flowers and blade.
It will have fire.

But before it burns,
I have yet to tell my last story,
lest other mouths
swallow the words in fear,
lest they choose the comfort
of lip-service to another tale.

Truth is too vulnerable
on the shrinking tongue.
Most times, it shrinks with it
and feigns disappearance.

Or it is made to cling
to the roof of the mouth.
The throat has to be cleared
with ease. But ease
is pure fancy unless words
step out of the lips,
as if there were no other place
to go, but out into the light.
I opt for ease, so I shall tell you
about the last days before tonight.

I slept with Ulap for two weeks,
and the Elders did not sleep.
Around their fire, they schemed
against my indiscretion.

FIRST ELDER:          Pagtuga should never know.

SECOND ELDER:         But how?

THIRD ELDER:          Her father allows
                      the earth to soil her bed.

FIRST ELDER:          Numb in his tongue,
                      he stares about more sullen
                      than ever. He now refuses
                      to consult with us.

THIRD ELDER:          Since the death of the slave,
                      he has left his hut
                      early each morning to hunt
                      with his best warriors.
                      Could it be that
                      he prepares for war?

| | |
|---|---|
| FIRST ELDER: | Who needs another war<br>for a whore who has forgotten<br>how to keep her knees together? |
| SECOND ELDER: | He is hunting for answers. |
| FIRST ELDER: | How can a voiceless chief have<br>answers? |
| THIRD ELDER: | Nameless as well.<br>He does not deserve his name.<br>Makusog — The Strong One. |
| FIRST ELDER: | Voiceless. Nameless.<br>Even his member has shrunk. |
| SECOND ELDER: | Do not forget that<br>we speak of our Datu. |
| FIRST ELDER: | Time to act against<br>the intruder on her bed.<br>What potion did he brew<br>to keep her on her back?<br>He must be dealt with quickly. |
| THIRD ELDER: | A simple task really.<br>What fight is there<br>in a kept man? |
| SECOND ELDER: | We must convince our Datu.<br>Pagtuga has just sent<br>his final word yesterday:<br>the Princess or war. |
| FIRST ELDER: | And our Datu kept silent? |
| SECOND ELDER: | No — he refused to give his<br>daughter. |

| | |
|---|---|
| THE ELDERS: | He has lost his mind, his name, his tongue! |
| DARAGANG MAGAYON: | My father sealed his lips since the murder of my nurse. His wordlessness slipped from his throne and sat around my chamber. It curled at the foot of the bed, where Ulap and I slept, like a cold draft nipping at my soles. |
| | Then, one bright morning, the *saya-saya* woke me with its ominous song. |
| YOUNG DARAGANG MAGAYON: | Can you hear it, Ulap? |
| ULAP: | A bird singing. |
| YOUNG DARAGANG MAGAYON: | A bird warning. |
| ULAP: | Trick of the ear. |
| YOUNG DARAGANG MAGAYON: | It is the deathtrill. Sirangan told me once about the *saya-saya*. Its song is an omen. |
| ULAP: | You have too many dark stories that are never told. |
| YOUNG DARAGANG MAGAYON: | Time to leave, my favoured one. The story seeks its end. |

| | |
|---|---|
| ULAP: | Untold story. |
| YOUNG DARAGANG MAGAYON: | It is my story. |
| ULAP: | As they were your songs which you kept me from singing that first time we met? |
| YOUNG DARAGANG MAGAYON: | I take from you only what you offer, and so should you — there it is again, the *saya-saya* at my window. You should go, Ulap. We have always known that this would be brief. The walls are growing mouths and they have teeth. |
| DARAGANG MAGAYON: | We woke to the portent stirrings of fear, anger and desire. I had never told him my stories, nor given reasons. But that morning, he begged for them. And the *saya-saya* sang on, while more mouths gashed my walls in a babble of urgency. |
| FIRST ELDER: | Daragang Magayon, leave that bed, and know the consequence of sleeping with the earth. |
| | And, listen, all of you. Pagtuga shall not take anything less than victory. |

| | |
|---|---|
| WOMEN: | His men captured our Datu? |
| First Warrior: | We tried to fight. |
| SECOND WARRIOR: | But we were outnumbered. |
| THIRD WARRIOR: | They demand the Princess. |
| SECOND WARRIOR: | She must marry him<br>within six days, or else,<br>it will be war. |
| YOUNG DARAGANG MAGAYON: | So the beast asks for war? |
| FIRST ELDER: | Here she comes,<br>glutted with desire. |
| SECOND ELDER: | Hush, there are other ears around. |
| FIRST ELDER: | How can you be so calm? |
| SECOND ELDER: | Your father has been taken. |
| FIRST ELDER: | Because of one whore! |
| FIRST WARRIOR: | We raised our swords, Princess,<br>but all for naught. |
| SECOND WARRIOR: | How to fight now<br>without a chief? |
| THIRD ELDER: | Why fight? The Princess<br>will appease Pagtuga.<br>She will bring her father back. |
| WOMEN: | No! Have you forgotten Sirangan?<br>Have you changed your minds<br>about the likes of Bakonawa? |

| | |
|---|---|
| THE ELDERS: | Would you prefer a war? |
| YOUNG DARAGANG MAGAYON: | I will bring my father back. Who wants to come with me to fight the monster in his lair? |
| THE ELDERS: | Will you listen to childish boldness? |
| THIRD WARRIOR: | But, Princess, there is no chief — |
| THE ELDERS: | And no certainty of winning. |
| FIRST WOMAN: | I shall go. Enough of this greed for young flesh! |
| FIRST ELDER: | Enough of war! You wish to lose sons again? |
| SECOND WOMAN: | I could go, but my only son is barely twelve — *ay,* my heart is torn apart. |
| THIRD WOMAN: | I detest war, but why swallow fear — I shall go. |
| FIRST ELDER: | *Ay,* poor woman, keep your heart around the hearth. More blood will only kill the fire. |
| SECOND ELDER: | A fair exchange is all they ask. One woman for peace. |

| | |
|---|---|
| THIRD ELDER: | Instead of a whole tribe in war. |
| SECOND WOMAN: | Not my remaining son —<br>no, I have seen too much death.<br>Daragang Magayon,<br>plead with Pagtuga.<br>Calm his wrath. |
| FIRST ELDER: | And marry him.<br>It is most simple. |
| FIRST WOMAN: | No! Another daughter<br>for the bed of the beast? |
| ULAP: | I shall not allow it! |
| WOMEN: | A man in her room? |
| YOUNG DARAGANG MAGAYON: | Meddle not, Ulap — |
| WARRIORS: | A stranger? |
| FIRST ELDER: | Not strange<br>to her bed. |
| SECOND ELDER: | Why must he appear?<br>All will smell the story out<br>and Pagtuga will know.<br>I sense the dying of the hearth. |
| WOMEN: | Who is he? |
| WARRIORS: | And why is he in the Princess'<br>chamber? |
| DARAGANG MAGAYON: | Agitation brewed into judgment.<br>In most eyes, I had whored |

with a stranger with no coil of cloth
around his head to prove his rank.
I read the verdict on most faces:
The Beautiful Maiden
who fed her maidenhood
to the nameless man
had sold her father
for a piece of lowly meat.

FIRST ELDER:          Waste no time — warriors,
                      take her to Pagtuga.

THIRD WOMAN:          *Ay*, what foolish choice is war!
                      We must keep Pagtuga happy.

YOUNG DARAGANG        How quick this change of mind.
MAGAYON:              Is it because of the man in my bed?

FIRST ELDER:          Warriors, why delay
                      your duty to our Datu?

YOUNG DARAGANG        Stand back.
MAGAYON:              Without my father,
                      I take command.
                      I swear by the blade,
                      I will bring him back.

SECOND ELDER:         What foolish willfulness.
                      Lost your better sense, Princess?

FIRST WARRIOR:        We wish not harm,
                      but common good.

SECOND WOMAN:         But will Pagtuga still desire
                      her who loses the scent
                      of *kadlum* leaves?

THIRD WOMAN:          *Ay*, Princess, why have you
                      taken this other man?

| | |
|---|---|
| FIRST WOMAN: | But we own and will our bodies.<br>Have you forgotten<br>the ritual by the sea? |
| ULAP: | I will bring you back your Datu.<br>I owe my life to your Princess. |
| THE ELDERS: | Shut up! You have spawned<br>enough doom with your loin.<br>Warriors! Take him prisoner. |
| YOUNG DARAGANG<br>MAGAYON: | Wait — I decide!<br>We will fight a common enemy,<br>not each other. Trust me. |
| FIRST ELDER: | I am the oldest man<br>in this tribe. Heed me. |
| WARRIORS: | It is only a marriage, Princess,<br>for the life of our tribe. |
| FIRST WOMAN: | We will feed her to Bakonawa?<br>She danced with us once. |
| THIRD WOMAN: | And waited with us<br>for our daughters —<br>but what choice have we<br>against the beast? |
| FIRST WOMAN: | Feed her to the moon-eater?<br>Why let him win? |
| SECOND WOMAN: | How could a tribe<br>that speaks against itself<br>now fight a war? |
| FIRST ELDER: | How could there be a war<br>if she were wise? |

| | |
|---|---|
| FIRST WOMAN: | What wiser move<br>than asking the *Kibang*?<br>Stupidly, we fight among ourselves<br>for what we cannot divine.<br>The oracle must tell us what to do. |
| WARRIORS: | Yes, the *Kibang*!<br>Ask the oracle! |
| WOMEN: | Draw the wisdom<br>from the navel of the sea. |
| DARAGANG MAGAYON: | Thus the pilgrimage to the shore<br>for the divination.<br>Dressed in warrior's gear,<br>I went to sea in a boat<br>without outriggers.<br>Then, with shield<br>poised above my head,<br>I called out —<br>'Should I marry Pagtuga?'<br>On the beach, the tribe<br>was as silent as the dead.<br><br>That hot summer noon,<br>the deep blue waters<br>turned green, grey,<br>then blue again,<br>changing hues as if forever.<br>As the boat began to rock,<br>the waves leapt into the colour<br>of fire — the seabed was<br>spitting from a furnace.<br><br>Cold yet burning,<br>those crests of flame<br>almost licking heaven.<br>Water-fire, fire-water<br>with a hundred fishes |

in its wake — talking fishes!
Each time they rose in a red swell,
they sang a folk riddle in one voice:
'What fish does not swim
against the current?'

Gentle at first,
then with an urgency,
an anger almost,
and soon a raving fury,
my lullaby for drowning —
'What fish does not swim
against the current?'
Fire-water-fishes-voices
expunging breath and hope.
My boat sank
into a burning pyre.

RED LAKE:            Did she answer the riddle?

GREEN LAKE:          Is she wise?

BLUE LAKE:           Did she answer the riddle?

GREEN LAKE:          Is she wise?

RED LAKE:            Did she answer the riddle?

MAGINDARA:           She will answer the riddle.
                     She is wise.

THE THREE LAKES:     What fish does not swim
                     against the current?

                     What fish does not swim
                     against the current?

MAGINDARA:           Hush. Let her be for a while.
                     Welcome to the belly of the earth.
                     This is Sirob, and I am Magindara.

DARAGANG MAGAYON:    I woke up on a huge burning stone
in the middle of three lakes,
red, green and blue in colour.
Beside me, the sea-goddess
whose creatures we once invoked,
shimmered the hues of the lakes.
Her brow and eyes were young,
but her mouth was old;
her long hair was grey
and waving strangely.

Fishes darted in
and out of the grey,
strands curled into
an anemone's tendrils
as corals playfully tugged
at their ends. Green breasts
winked their saltwhite nipples.
Red fins for hips quivered,
and arms became wings
when raised, then arms again
as they flapped.

And what stone for a navel!
Evening black, but mirroring all,
thus winking every colour.
Her pubis, crimson flowers,
and her legs, water flowing
toward the three lakes,
as if she were endlessly
filling them with her hues —
she began to dance.

MAGINDARA:    You will be old and young
with my years and colours
as I dance your dance.

I am you now — watch me.
I watched you for years.

I heard you remember me
as you remembered
your sea-lives.

I watched your mothers, too.
I listened to their memories
of my world in their bodies.
I heard them sing with you.

RED LAKE:          Eyes splinterless as the moon.

MAGINDARA:         What fish does not swim
                   against the current?

GREEN LAKE:        Lips to fruit with words.

MAGINDARA:         What fish does not swim
                   against the current?

BLUE LAKE:         Breasts without the welts.

MAGINDARA:         What fish does not swim
                   against the current?

DARAGANG MAGAYON:  'A dead fish?' I replied.
                   'Why answer a riddle
                   with a question. Must you doubt?'
                   The three lakes scolded,
                   but Magindara hushed them
                   and resumed her dance.
                   She plucked her navel
                   and swallowed it.
                   Her belly swelled darkly,
                   as if the stone grew
                   inside her, as if she were
                   pregnant with its night.

                   Her red flowers opened.
                   Hooves pushed out

between her legs,
then the ebony form
of a long-limbed monster
with lips swollen
on a horse face! What grace —
it pranced about
continuing her rhythm.

This half-man, half-stallion
picked her up,
and swallowed her whole.
Wrapping his limbs
around me, he neighed,
'I am the Tambaluslus.'
Then he drank from the green river
and began to spit a reptilian tail
scaled with topazes.

Tail that grew a waist,
breasts, arms, neck, head —
a yellow snake-woman
curling and uncurling
in the tempo of the dance!
One yellow ripple,
and she devoured the man-horse,
then turned to me, singing,
'I am Oryol of the forest.'

Wound around my waist,
she lay her head upon my breast,
the hiss of a song
intimate with my heart.
Then she began to fade —
I was alone on the red stone,
but not quite, because a voice
whispered, 'I am the Tawong-lipod,
always The Unseen.'

From where the voice came,
a dwarf leapt to my shoulder,
screeching another name, 'Luwok!
Luwok!' with such frenzy,
as he grew back
the long grey hair,
the young-old face,
the red-green-blue body
dance-shimmering.
Magindara was back.

MAGINDARA:            I am beyond fish, coral,
anemone or stone.
I am also the beast
swallowing myself.
I am fire. I am darkness.
I am what you love
and what you fear.
I can make you live,
yet I can kill.

I am Magindara,
yet not quite Magindara.
I am Tambaluslus, Oryol,
Tawong-lipod, Luwok,
but none of them.

And what of you?
What is your name?

THE THREE LAKES:      Daragang Magayon.

MAGINDARA:            What is your name?

THE THREE LAKES:      Sadit ni Makusog.

MAGINDARA:            What is your name?

THE THREE LAKES:      Agomon ni Pagtuga.

| | |
|---|---|
| MAGINDARA: | What is your name? |
| | Answer not. |
| | You are nameless.<br>Yet you own all names. |
| THE THREE LAKES: | Warang Pangaran<br>Na Kagsadiri Kang Gabos Na<br>Pangaran. |
| | Warang Pangaran<br>Na Kagsadiri Kang Gabos Na<br>Pangaran. |
| DARAGANG MAGAYON: | The three lakes chanted,<br>flooding the red stone<br>with waterwords,<br>washing me and Magindara<br>off our feet, sweeping me<br>away from her.<br>I found myself swimming,<br>rising from the navel of the sea,<br>as the chanting of names went on. |
| WOMEN: | Daragang Magayon! |
| | Come back, O Wandering Soul! |
| | Sadit ni Makusog! |
| | Come back, O Wandering Soul! |
| FIRST WOMAN: | But she cannot be dead. |
| SECOND WOMAN: | Like her father. |
| THIRD WOMAN: | You mean — ? He was still alive<br>when they found him by the river. |

SECOND WOMAN:    We could not stem the blood
                 ebbing from his wish to live.
                 He kept crying for his daughter
                 and Dawani. He escaped Pagtuga,
                 but not his fate.

THIRD WOMAN:     First, the Datu —
                 and now the Princess?

FIRST WOMAN:     No! Call out her names again.

THIRD WOMAN:     But we have done so for days.

FIRST WOMAN:     Call then for the other names
                 that we remembered on the beach.

                 Call out all her names —

                 Fish! Rise with the waves!

                 Coral! Beach on the sand!

                 Bird! Wing to our voice!

SECOND WOMAN:    How still she is.

THIRD WOMAN:     Tight-fisted spirits would not
                 release her from the dead.

SECOND WOMAN:    We should not have had the *Kibang*.
                 Oracles can kill —

FIRST WOMAN:     Hush, all of you.
                 Her lips are moving.

DARAGANG MAGAYON: Warang Pangaran.
                 Warang Pangaran.

SECOND WOMAN:    Nameless One?

190

| | |
|---|---|
| DARAGANG MAGAYON: | Kagsadiri Kang Gabos Na Pangaran. |
| THIRD WOMAN: | Who Owns All Names? |
| SECOND WOMAN: | Look, her hair is turning grey! |
| THIRD WOMAN: | And her face is young but old! |
| SECOND WOMAN: | Her hands are burning fire! |
| THIRD WOMAN: | Is it she? |
| SECOND WOMAN: | Perhaps, a stray spirit. |

FIRST WOMAN:  No! Watch —
her hair is darkening.
Her face is young again.
And the fires are dying.
It is she. She is alive!

DARAGANG MAGAYON:  Before the sun had set yesterday,
I woke up on my bed,
the women around me
weeping and laughing
in aborted grief.
They said I had drowned
during the *Kibang*,
that they tried to revive me
for five days in the ritual
of the *Sakom*. My soul
had wandered,
but they called it back.

Then the Elders came to my hut.
Father has returned,
they said, averting eyes.
They led me to his bed.
How very pale and silent
as he stared at me.

I searched the blankness
of his gaze for something
beyond death —
something close to love.
But the Elders closed his lids.

Then they turned to me,
asking for the wisdom
of the oracle. I had to swallow
the tides in my throat;
no time for grief.
The story must be told:
When I asked,
'Should I marry Pagtuga?'
the reply was an old riddle.
'What fish does not swim
against the current?'

*Ay,* we are not dead fishes.
Thus, each woman, man and child
gripped the blade
close to a warrior's heart,
and Ulap did the same.
Again, he must meet
the enemy. So he waits
with us, even as they
eye him with suspicion.

Now, we are only a handspan
away from the rearing
spectre of a battlefield,
prelude to the grave.
It will be soon, very soon.
The east is swallowing the dark
with its vicious hunger
from a long night's fast.
In a while, it will spit out fishes
that are all eyes of the sun,
as we endlessly turn

in the inevitable dance
on the red stone.

Since last night,
we have not stopped
pounding it with soles
that sing of fire. Listen —

we pound the red to rage.

Faster each turn —

but wait!

Is this rhythm of feet

dancing?

Or running — ?

They have come!
The north teems
with Pagtuga's spawn.

Blow the *hamodyong*!

Pluck the black navel!

Let them race to a bloodbath!

*Ay,* but what a day to die —

this half-light
is too beautiful for war!

## EPILOGUE

*Cantata of the Mountain*

Flight is song
on four winds
From the east,
a voice is red-
rimmed with fire.
From the west,
it gusts grey
with ashes.

Flight is song
on four winds.
From the north,
a voice is sea-
weed green.
From the south,
it gales into
a startling blue.

Flight is song
on four winds
of fire-and-ashes-
sea-and-sky-
slumberered tomb.
Scale this mound
of pearlboned lovers
in my womb.

This was the grave after that war,
this mountain of fire
that rose from all our bodies
gathered by those who lived.

(*I shall know you earth
more than mountain fire.*)

No great funeral. No coloured jars.
No chanting. Only a hush,
a tired lull for tending wounds.

(*I shall know you
in that firmest breast
stunning me to a flash of wing.*)

The tribe of Rawis bore the sun.
We killed Pagtuga,
felled fifty strong
in a two-day fight.

(*You lift me aching with desire.*)

But for every life we took,
we lost two. In a single heave,
we wielded our freedom
from fear of the beast.

(*Ay, this smouldering of eyes.*)

But how we died —
women, men, children
turned beasts as well,
and out for blood.

(*This acheful kindling of the thighs.*)

Rawis was the red stone,
the belly-rhythm
of this volcano that rose
from a deathdance.

(*Is this the peak?*)

Look closely then
at this mound of earth
that you ask for beauty.

(*This strangest crest?*)

This is the ascent of rage
and grief of a whole tribe.

(*This hideous breast?*)

So how dare you demand
that it be smooth and firm
as a breast without history?
I am also the song that aches
to rise between the thighs
of men before any battle.
I am the womb that throbs
between desire and death.
I am the mouth remembering
the coupled heaving of women
and men in another passion
called a war.

I am deeply furrowed
by the universal scar.
My wounds are not mine alone.
Neither is my fire.
Pass your memory
like a seeking palm
over your vision.
*Ay*, the whiteness of your eyes
also runs red trails.
Let me prance on them
and trace where they begin.

## Reply to the Mountain

I am tired of long stories.
I need to go back to the womb
where I can dream
of breasts that do not speak.
Only warm and full
with generous nipples
brownpink with life.
What need is there
for your stories?
I write history.

Eyes are not for mapping out
my vision. These red trails
are not yours to trace.
Tell your stories in another time.
Sing your songs for ready ears.
Too steep your scales,
octaves beyond hills.
And I am tired.
I need to sleep tonight.

### Coda of the Mountain

But before a battle once,
I told my stories
to the night with ears,
which was also your night.
Now, I tell my stories again,
but tonight is for your stupor,
blind and sweet. Your lids
have shut to hide your eye-trails.
You snuggle close to your history:

*The mountain of Mayon*
*carved from the name*
*Daragang Magayon.*
*Daughter of Datu Makusog.*
*Accepted marriage*
*from Pagtuga to save*
*her father and keep*
*the peace of the tribe.*
*Rescued by Ulap, her lover,*
*who fought Pagtuga.*
*Died from a spear*
*hurled by the enemy.*
*Buried. Her tomb rose*
*into a mountain of fire.*

Your mock history coddles you
and your desires
with jealous night-arms
while you sleep.
*Ay,* you give me reasons for war,
even as I wish to rest
in blue-grey-green,
shades of sea-creatures
I once have been,
yet promising the black stone.
You give me reasons
to keep my promise.

You rush me to its wake.
You have just spurred
the ancient feet to beat
the red stone again.
You have called upon Rawis
to brew the song of fire.
You have willed the hands
to pluck the black navel.
Watch my mouth then
swallowing the dark
and spitting redly the sun.

Flight is song
on four winds.
The fifth wind
does not sing.

Flight is song
on four winds.
the fifth wind
does not sing.

## MERLINDA BOBIS' POETRY PERFORMANCES

**PROMENADE** (*excerpts*)

*1997*

Illawarra Carnivale, Wollongong City Gallery, 12 September

Perth Writers' Festival, Fremantle, Perth, 2 March

*1995*

World Forum on Women, China, 7 September

Art of Lunch, Music Centre, University of Wollongong, May

Varuna Writers' Centre, Katoomba, February

**CANTATA OF THE WARRIOR WOMAN
DARAGANG MAGAYON**

*1998*

ABC 'The Listening Room', 6 April

*1996*

Darwin Arts Festival (with film projections by Virginia Hilyard),
26–28 August

*1995*

Paco Park Presents (as guest artist for Concert at the Park),
Manila, 22 September

NGO World Forum on Women, Beijing, China, 5–6 September

Australia Centre, Manila, 1 July

Habi, On To Beijing Concert, University of the Philippines,
Manila, 24 June

### 1994

Asian Theatre Festival 1994, Belvoir Street Theatre, Sydney,
    22–23 September
Wongi Wongi (A Festival of Women's Writing), Perth, 6 August
6th International Feminist Book Fair, Melbourne, 30–31 July
3rd International Women Playwrights Conference, Adelaide,
    9 July
Philippine–France Festival, Paris, 19–20 May
Cultural Centre of the Philippines, Manila, 18–19, 22–23 February

### 1993

Stables Theatre, Sydney, 24 October
Women in Asia Conference, Melbourne University, 1 October
Spring Writing, NSW Writing Centre, Sydney, 19 September
Cultural Centre of the Philippines, Manila, 7 September
Bicol University Theatre, Legaspi City, Philippines, 30 August
Performance Space, Faculty of Creative Arts, University of
    Wollongong, 28, 30 July
Regional Poetry Festival, Wollongong City Gallery, 12 June
Sydney Writers Festival, NSW Library, 25 January
Faculty of Arts & Letters, University of Santo Tomas, 9 January

### 1992

Intercontinental Hotel, Manila, 19 December
Conference of Folk Healers, Batangas, Philippines, 7 December
Art of Lunch, School of Creative Arts, University of Wollongong,
    29 October
Writers In the Park, Harold Park Hotel, Sydney, 8 September
Postgraduate Open Day, University of Wollongong, 14 August
Philippine Studies International Conference, Australian National
    University, Canberra, 2 July
Wollongong City Gallery, 16 June

# OTHER POETRY TITLES FROM SPINIFEX PRESS

**Suniti Namjoshi**
**Feminist Fables**

An ingenious reworking of fairytales. Mythology, mixed with the author's original material and vivid imagination. An indispensible feminist classic.
*Her imagination soars to breathtaking heights . . . she has the enviable skill of writing stories that are as entertaining as they are thought-provoking.*
Kerry Lyon, *Australian Book Review*
ISBN 1 875559 19 1

## St Suniti and the Dragon

Ironic and fantastic, elegant and elegaic, fearful and funny. A thoroughly modern fable.
*I can think of plenty of adjectives to describe St Suniti and the Dragon, but not a noun to go with them. It's hilarious, witty, elegantly written, hugely inventive, fantastic, energetic . . . With work as original as this, it's easier to fling words at it than to say what it is or what it does.* U. A. Fanthorpe
ISBN 1 875559 18 3

## Building Babel

"Come and play," invites Suniti Namjoshi, "Building Babel is what people do." A fabulous new book in which time, power and the discipline of love come under scrutiny.
*Suniti Namjoshi is an inspired fabulist: she asks the difficult questions — about good and evil, about nature and war — unfailingly bracing her readers with her mordant humor and the lively play of her imagination.*
Marina Warner

Do you want to be published on the Internet? Then visit the Babel Building Site at
<http://www.publishaust.net.au/~spinifexbabelbuildingsite.html> and send your contributions to Spinifex.
ISBN 1 875559 56 6

**Gillian Hanscombe**
**Sybil: The Glide of Her Tongue**

*A book where the lesbian voice meditates the essential vitality of she-dykes who have visions. A book where Gillian Hanscombe's poetry opens up meaning in such a way that it provides for beauty and awareness, for a space where one says yes to a lesbian we of awareness.* Nicole Brossard
*O I am enamoured of Sybil. Gillian Hanscombe is one of the most insightfully ironic, deliciously lyrical voices we have writing amongst us today.*
Betsy Warland

ISBN 1 875559 05 1

**Diane Fahey**
**The Body in Time**
*Diane Fahey pieces together a world – with integrity and incomparable delicacy – much as the fragile light of a star defines a universe.*
Annie Greet

**Jordie Albiston**
**Nervous Arcs**
*Jordie Albiston writes with sharp intelligence, lyrical grace, and moral passion. A name to watch for.* Janette Turner Hospital
Winner, Mary Gilmore Award, 1996
Second Prize, Anne Elder FAW Award, 1996
ISBN 1 875559 37 X

**Louise Crisp**
**Ruby Camp**
*Crisp's insights and perceptions are so original and intense that she has needed to find a new language, precise and sensuous, mysterious and revealing, held in a fine balance of rhythm and phrasing. She creates a radically new way of 'knowing' the East Gippsland bush: "strong as illusion the dream works/ its way into landscape". It is finally a book about joy.*
Marie Tulip

**Miriel Lenore**
**Travelling Alone Together**
Three journeys across the Nullarbor and time are interwoven as Lenore explores our myths.
*This poet/traveller is incredibly modest and respectful of what is given her to experience. She travels across her many landscapes naming without appropriating.*
Alison Clark
ISBN 1 875559 83 3

## Robyn Rowland
## Perverse Serenity

What happens when an Australian feminist falls in love with an Irish monk? Daring, passionate and forceful poetry about the limits of love and obsession.

*Here is writing not afraid to be vulnerable, not trapped in literary artifice, not reticent about emotion, its hopes, its fears, its withdrawals and assertions, which we all share and which enrich our humanity.*

Barret Reid

ISBN 1 875559 13 2

## Sandy Jeffs
## Poems from the Madhouse

*This is disturbing but quite wonderful poetry, because of its clarity, its humour, its imagery, and the insights it gives us into being human, being mad, being sane. I read and read – and was profoundly moved. I delighted in it as poetry; I was touched by its honesty, courage and vulnerability.*
Anne Deveson

*The language challenges her with fifty names for madness, writing of a life of vigilance and struggle, she enlarges our understanding of human capacity.*
Judith Rodriguez

Certificate of Commendation, Human Rights Award for Poetry, 1994
Second Prize, Anne Elder FAW Award, 1994

## Deborah Staines
## Now Millennium

*Deborah Staines' respect for and awareness of language's dynamic possibilities bring inner and outer worlds attentively alive.* Fay Zwicky
*This book is really wild . . . There's so much passion and commitment there and she's drunk with words.*
Dorothy Hewett

Winner, Mary Gilmore Award, 1994

ISBN 1 875559 20 5

*If you would like to know more about Spinifex Press,*
*write for a free catalogue or visit our Home Page.*

**SPINIFEX PRESS**
PO Box 212, North Melbourne,
Victoria 3051, Australia
http://www.spinifexpress.com.au/~women